This holiday season, Whitehorn has more than its share of troubles: Who's laundering money through the Hip Hop Café? Why does new Hip Hop waitress Darcy Montague stash thousands of dollars in her music box? And what's eating Homer Gilmore? Join some new as well as familiar faces for Yuletide excitement and, as always, true love!

CAST OF CHARACTERS

Mark Kincaid: A cop who has worked the beat on New York City's streets and comes home for some peace and quiet. He'll never be anyone's fool again. But is he too tough to fall for his adorable neighbor, Darcy Montague?

Darcy Montague: A baker and waitress, Darcy can't keep a thought in her head while ogling drop-dead-gorgeous customer Mark Kincaid. When he starts to show interest, can she protect her secret responsibility—or her vulnerable heart?

Homer Gilmore: The man wanders around town in his bathrobe and slippers, lost in his own world—but carries a burden that no one can see. Does he know the person who's been causing trouble around Whitehorn this holiday season?

Josh Anderson: What is this sexy bachelor doing sniffing around Whitehorn's cutest new waitress? *Nothing,* as far as Mark's concerned!

Melissa North: Can the owner of the Hip Hop Café possibly be involved in the mysterious laundering scheme Mark Kincaid is reluctantly investigating?

Nurse Connie Adams: As Homer's caregiver, what is she doing letting Homer run loose around town? And why is she making eyes at Melissa's husband?

Dear Reader,

'Tis the season to ask yourself "What makes Christmas special?" (other than a Silhouette Special Edition novel in your stocking, that is). For Susan Mallery, it's "sharing in established traditions and starting new ones." And what could be more of a tradition than reading Susan's adorable holiday MONTANA MAVERICKS story, *Christmas in Whitehorn?*

Peggy Webb's statement of the season, "The only enduring gift is love" resonates in us all as she produces an enduring gift with *The Smile of an Angel* from her series THE WESTMORELAND DIARIES. Along with love, author Patricia Kay feels that Christmas "is all about joy—the joy of being with family and loved ones." And we are overjoyed to bring you the latest in her CALLAHANS & KIN miniseries, *Just a Small-Town Girl.*

Sylvie Kurtz shows us the "magical quality" of the holidays in *A Little Christmas Magic*, a charming opposites-attract love story. And we are delighted by Patricia McLinn's *My Heart Remembers* from her WYOMING WILDFLOWERS miniseries. For Patricia, "Christmas is family. Revisiting memories, but also focusing on today." Crystal Green echoes this thought. "The word *family* is synonymous with Christmas." So curl up with her latest, *The Pregnant Bride*, from her new miniseries, KANE'S CROSSING!

As you can see, we have many talented writers to celebrate this holiday season in Special Edition.

Happy Holidays!

Karen Taylor Richman
Senior Editor

Please address questions and book requests to:
Silhouette Reader Service
U.S.: 3010 Walden Ave., P.O. Box 1325, Buffalo, NY 14269
Canadian: P.O. Box 609, Fort Erie, Ont. L2A 5X3

Susan Mallery

Christmas in Whitehorn

SPECIAL EDITION™

Published by Silhouette Books
America's Publisher of Contemporary Romance

Special thanks and acknowledgment are given to Susan Mallery for her contribution to the MONTANA MAVERICKS series.

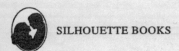 SILHOUETTE BOOKS

ISBN 0-373-24435-5

CHRISTMAS IN WHITEHORN

Books by Susan Mallery

Silhouette Special Edition

Tender Loving Care #717
More Than Friends #802
A Dad for Billie #834
Cowboy Daddy #898
*The Best Bride #933
*Marriage on Demand #939
*Father in Training #969
*The Bodyguard &
  Ms. Jones* #1008
*Part-Time Wife #1027
Full-Time Father #1042
*Holly and Mistletoe #1071
*Husband by the Hour #1099
†The Girl of His Dreams #1118
†The Secret Wife #1123
†The Mysterious Stranger #1130
The Wedding Ring Promise #1190
Prince Charming, M.D. #1209
The Millionaire Bachelor #1220
‡Dream Bride #1231
‡Dream Groom #1244
Beth and the Bachelor #1263
Surprise Delivery #1273
A Royal Baby on the Way #1281
*A Montana Mavericks Christmas:
  "Married in Whitehorn"* #1286
Their Little Princess #1298
**The Sheik's Kidnapped Bride #1316
**The Sheik's Arranged Marriage #1324
**The Sheik's Secret Bride #1331
‡‡The Rancher Next Door #1358
‡‡Unexpectedly Expecting! #1370
‡‡Wife in Disguise #1383
Shelter in a Soldier's Arms #1400
**The Sheik and the Runaway Princess #1430
Christmas in Whitehorn #1435

Silhouette Intimate Moments

Tempting Faith #554
The Only Way Out #646
Surrender in Silk #770
Cinderella for a Night #1029

Silhouette Books

36 Hours
*The Rancher and the
  Runaway Bride*

Montana Mavericks Weddings
"Cowgirl Bride"

World's Most Eligible Bachelors
Lone Star Millionaire

Harlequin Books

Montana Mavericks:
  Big Sky Grooms
  "Spirit of the Wolf"

Harlequin Historicals

Justin's Bride #270
Wild West Wife #419
Shotgun Grooms #575
"Lucas's Convenient Bride"

*Hometown Heartbreakers
†Triple Trouble
‡Brides of Bradley House
**Desert Rogues
‡‡Lone Star Canyon

SUSAN MALLERY

is the bestselling author of over forty-five books for Harlequin Books and Silhouette Books. She makes her home in the Pacific Northwest with her handsome prince of a husband and her two adorable-but-not-bright cats.

Mark Kincaid had no business being there.

"Look, Darcy—"

Mark paused, not sure how to tell her he wouldn't make it for dinner. He wasn't very social these days.

Her blue eyes stared at him, while the corners of her full mouth turned up slightly. She had perfect skin. Clear, pale and nearly luminous. But the worst of it was the complete trust in her eyes. He had a bad feeling that she'd never told a white lie, let alone a really soul-threatening one. He felt like he was about to kick a puppy.

His shoulders slumped. "Do you want me to bring anything? Like wine?"

"Wine would be nice," she said.

He nodded and left without looking at her. He didn't want to see her smiling at him like he'd just done something amazing. However much he found Darcy attractive, he wasn't about to go there. As he'd already learned the hard way, getting involved with a woman could be fatal.

Chapter One

"**W**estern omelette, side of bacon, coffee," Mark Kincaid said without looking up from his morning paper. He hadn't slept the night before and he felt like roadkill. Of course he hadn't *been* sleeping since the shooting, so he should stop being surprised by the fact. Maybe one day he would get used to staring up at the ceiling for hours on end, trying *not* to relive the events that had nearly killed him.

"I don't think so."

At first he thought he'd imagined the soft voice, that the words were an editorial on his belief he might get used to not sleeping. Then he realized they'd come from the petite blonde standing next to his table.

He looked up at the waitress smiling at him. He didn't smile in return. "Excuse me?"

"I said no. You can't order that for breakfast. You

get the same thing every day and it's not healthy. Four eggs, ham, cheese *and* bacon? It's enough cholesterol to choke a horse.''

"Fortunately, I'm not a horse.''

Her smile widened. Humor danced in her eyes. "Good point, Detective. Okay, it's enough cholesterol to clog the arteries of a living human. How about some oatmeal? Studies have proven that regular consumption of oatmeal can actually lower cholesterol levels, sometimes significantly.''

Mark folded his paper and gave the waitress his full attention. She wore a white apron over a pale pink dress. Two butterfly clips held her short blond hair away from her face. She was pretty enough, he supposed, assuming a man was interested in that sort of thing. He was not.

He pushed his coffee cup closer to the edge of the table. She took the hint and filled it. He sipped the black liquid, nearly sighing when he felt it burn its way down his throat. Coffee improved his world view.

"Western omelette," he said firmly. "Side of bacon."

Her full lips pressed together. "How about a side of fruit, instead? It's fresh.''

He stared at her, giving her the same look he'd used on the scum of the earth he'd encountered while he'd been a detective in New York. The waitress— Darcy her name tag read—should have run for cover. Instead she muttered something about some people being too stubborn for their own good and wrote on her pad.

"I have to tell you, I'm giving in against my better judgment," she told him.

"What happened to 'the customer is always right'?"

"Being right won't help you if you're dead."

She sounded too damn cheerful by half.

"It's a little early for such a philosophical discussion," he said. "Why don't you save it for the lunch crowd?"

She smiled. "Let me guess—you won't be in for lunch today, right?"

He shrugged. He *did* have plans elsewhere.

"I'll put this right in," she said, waving her pad, then turning on her heel and heading for the kitchen.

Mark returned his attention to his paper, but the words didn't make sense. Instead he found himself trying to remember what, if anything, he knew about Darcy the waitress. She was new in town. She'd shown up in the eight years he'd been gone. She was young, early twenties, attractive—not that he cared about that—and a born fusser. She bullied all her customers equally, touting the benefits of orange juice with its vitamin C, warning kids about cavities from sticky desserts and pushing salads instead of burgers. Everyone seemed to love the attention. Everyone but him.

Mark shook his head to clear it, then studied the paper in front of him. Gradually the room faded as he reviewed the scores from the previous day's football games. Maybe this year the Dallas Cowboys were going to go all the way. Maybe—

A small plate appeared in front of him. Three slices of something strange lay nestled against each other.

He glanced at Darcy.

"Don't bite my head off. It's compliments of the house," she said casually. "We're considering switching suppliers for our baked goods. This is a sample of one of the new products. What do you think?"

The slices had come from a loaf of some kind. But the color was faintly...orange? "What is it?"

"Pumpkin bread."

He pushed the plate away. "I don't eat vegetables before noon."

Darcy glared at him as if he'd just won first prize in a stupid contest. "There are green peppers in your omelette. Besides, pumpkins aren't vegetables."

"Want to bet?"

"Okay, technically they are because of the seeds and everything, but we eat them in pie. That makes them an honorary fruit. Try it. It's really good."

He had his doubts. "Why pumpkin bread?"

"Because of Thanksgiving. It's this Thursday. Remember?"

He didn't remember, mostly because he didn't do holidays. Not anymore. When it had been only him and Maddie, he'd worked hard to make the holidays special. His sister had just been a kid when they'd lost their folks. But lately...what was the point?

"So the restaurant will be closed," he said, not asking a question. He'd have to fix his own breakfast. Actually, he'd probably not bother with food. Cooking was too much trouble.

Darcy's gaze narrowed. "Tell me, Detective, what exactly are your plans for the holiday?"

"Is my order ready yet?"

She nodded her head. "I knew it. You're the solitary type, aren't you? You'll spend the day by yourself, moping."

He glared at her. "I don't mope."

"But you *will* be alone."

He waved at the half-full Hip Hop Café. "Don't you have other customers?"

She glanced around. "Not really, but thanks for asking. My point is, no one should spend the holidays alone. You need to get out."

He was saved by the bell—literally. The sharp ring cut through the diner and sent Darcy back toward the kitchen. Less than a minute later she appeared with his breakfast.

"I mean it," she said. "Solitude makes the holidays more difficult than they have to be. Don't you have any family in town?"

He thought about his sister, who would spend the long weekend traveling. "No."

"Then come to my place. I'm fixing a turkey with all the trimmings. Everything is homemade. There will be lots of people there. You'll love it. You won't even have to talk if you don't want to. Although it wouldn't hurt you to be a tad more chatty, if you ask me."

He groaned. The last thing he needed was to fall into the clutches of some health-nut do-gooder. She'd probably use tofu in her stuffing and want to talk about the importance of giving back to the community.

He opened his mouth to refuse her invitation, but she was gone. Seconds later, she reappeared with coffee, pouring quickly, then leaving.

For the next ten minutes, she took care of her other customers, argued about what they were ordering and avoided Mark's table. He had plenty of time to think up fifteen reasons he would refuse her invitation. Yet when she brought him his bill, he found himself unable to say anything to bring sadness to her bright, expectant smile.

"What time?" he asked, trying to sound gracious and failing miserably.

Her expression turned startled. "You're accepting?"

"Change your mind already?"

"No. Not at all. Say four? We'll eat at five." She hesitated. "Do you know where I live?" Instantly she blushed. "Dumb question."

For the first time that day, possibly for the first time in several days, Mark smiled. "Yeah, Darcy. I know where you live."

Darcy Montague leaned her head against the front of her locker and groaned. The good news was she could now nominate herself for idiot of the month. What on earth had she been thinking?

"Please don't tell me that you're banging your head against the wall," Janie Carson Austin, who managed the Hip Hop, said as she stepped into the small storeroom. "You're one of my most dependable staff members and if I think you're going off the deep end, it's going to put a crimp in my holiday spirit.''

Darcy straightened and forced herself to smile at her boss. ''No head banging. I promise. Just a reflection on the state of my life.''

''Which is?'' Janie asked.

''Great.''

Darcy ignored the voice in her head—even though it was telling her she was incredibly dumb for inviting Mark Kincaid to her house. *Mark Kincaid*—Whitehorn's answer to Brad Pitt and Tom Cruise all rolled into one. Argh! Had she actually told him he didn't have to talk to anyone while he was at her house, only to turn around and complain that he wasn't chatty enough? She'd babbled. It had been humiliating.

Janie leaned against the door frame. ''Your pumpkin bread was a big hit. Maybe we should try something else next week.''

Instantly Darcy's spirits lifted. ''Thanks, Janie. I'll come up with something special. I really appreciate you giving me this opportunity.''

Janie, a pretty, blond thirty-year-old, shrugged. ''I try to be loyal to our longtime vendors, but I also owe our customers the best. If your next offering is as good as this one, and if the price is reasonable, I'm going to recommend we buy our baked goods from you.''

''I won't let you down,'' Darcy promised.

''I have every confidence in you,'' Janie said, and left.

Darcy gave a silent cheer as she sat on the skinny

bench in front of the lockers. *I have every confidence in you.* Who would have thought she would ever hear those words? For a long time she hadn't believed them herself. But now they were true. She was dependable, reliable and all those other lovely "able" words. Not bad for a former flake.

She was nearly as excited about the compliment as about the chance to expand business for Darcy's Delectables. If she could land a contract with the Hip Hop Café, she would go a long way toward building up her minuscule savings account. Life was definitely taking a turn for the better.

Which meant she could indulge in a back-patting festival if she wanted...or she could deal with her more pressing problem, namely the fact that she'd invited Mark Kincaid over for Thanksgiving.

Her good mood did an instant crash and burn. It wasn't that she objected to having the man in her house. How could she? He was easy on the eye in a big way. Of course that was also part of the problem. She hadn't been on a date in five years. To be blunt, the man turned her on. The combination of great body, killer green eyes and sexy, barely there smile was pure temptation. Something she had no time for right now.

To make matters worse, he was completely single. And from what she could tell, he didn't date. Not that she spied on him or anything, but he *did* live next door to her. They shared a duplex on the far side of town. He'd moved in a couple of months after she had, and what with him being so very good-looking, he'd been impossible to miss. She didn't exactly monitor his movements, but she was the tiniest bit aware of his comings and goings.

It was a crush. There—she'd admitted it to herself. She had a crush on him and that's what had her scared. What if he figured it out? She would be too humiliated to live, and right now she couldn't afford to die.

"I won't be alone," she reminded herself as she rose and headed back to the diner. Eight other people were going to be at her place for dinner on Thanksgiving. She would barely notice Mark's presence. With a large people-buffer in place, she might even avoid making a fool of herself in front of him.

"I really hate to cancel on such short notice," Millie Jasper said the following morning. She tried to sound sad, but instead she beamed with pleasure.

"I understand," Darcy said, because she *really* did understand. She just didn't like it very much. "If your parents want you to come home for the holidays, that's a whole lot better than staying here."

Millie shifted two-year-old Ronnie to her other hip. "I'm hoping they're going to ask me to move back home," she confided. "Ever since Ron ran off with that bimbo of his, I've been struggling. So this is like a miracle."

Darcy knew that miracles didn't come around very often. She patted her friend's arm. "Go home. Make peace with your parents and see if you can start over. I'll miss you on Thanksgiving, but this is better."

"Thanks for being so sweet."

Millie gave her a quick hug, which meant Ronnie

wanted to plant a sticky kiss on Darcy's cheek. Then the two of them waved goodbye as they left the café.

"Don't panic," Darcy murmured to herself. She reached for a clean cloth and began wiping off the counter. "There are still four other people coming to dinner."

Four people, plus *him*. Because she was now refusing to think about Mark Kincaid by name. Her insides had started acting very strange when she pictured him or said his name—her heart thumping when she thought about him, her stomach sort of heaving and swaying. It was scary and gross.

"I'm just doing a good deed," she reminded herself. "There's absolutely nothing personal going on."

It was a darned pitiful excuse for a lie.

Light snow fell Tuesday night as Mark jogged up the driveway toward the duplex. He'd pushed himself too far and felt the resulting pain in his side. With each step, still-healing muscles tugged and pulled, making him ache. He would pay for the extra miles in the morning when he would awaken stiff and sore. Assuming he slept.

At least he could go running and suffer the consequences, he reminded himself as he rounded the bend in the path. There'd been a time when he hadn't been sure he was even going to survive. Now he knew he would completely heal and—except for a few scars and a slightly more cynical take on the world—life would go on as it had before. Or would it? Could he ever trust a woman again...after what Sylvia had done to him?

He shook his head to clear it of thoughts of her. The driveway widened, circling in front of the single-story duplex. He was about to head to his half when he noticed his neighbor standing by her car, wrestling with something large in the back seat.

He slowed his steps. This wasn't his problem, he reminded himself. Living next door to someone didn't obligate him to anything. He stopped about ten feet from her car—her very *old* car. The compact import had seen better days and too many miles. There were chips in the green paint, a few rust spots and a battered rear fender. But the snow tires were new. At least Darcy knew enough to keep herself safe as winter approached.

She wrapped her arms around whatever was stuck in the back seat and tried to straighten. Instead she staggered back a couple of steps. Mark hurried forward before he could stop himself and grabbed the thing from her. The "it" in question turned out to be a very large, squishy turkey.

Darcy blinked at him.

"Mark. Hi."

A blue down jacket made her large eyes turn the color of a summer sky. Snow dotted her blond curls, and her ever-present smile widened.

"Thanks for the rescue." She waved at the turkey he held awkwardly against his chest. "I know it's too big, but I had to special-order it—you know, to get a fresh one. And it was either some puny thing or something large enough to feed the multitudes. My oven is huge, so I figured I'd just go for it. I know about a million ways to serve leftover turkey, so I don't mind if we don't eat it all on Thanksgiving.'' She paused to draw breath. "I know fresh turkeys are more expensive, plus this one was open-range raised, but it's only once a year, you know?''

The chilly bird had to weigh over twenty pounds. He could feel something wet dripping down his leg. Great.

"You want to show me where this goes?'' he asked.

"Oh. Sorry.''

She hurried toward the front door, glancing at him over her shoulder. "I could carry that. I mean you don't have to bring it in if you don't want to.''

He was nearly a foot taller and had to outweigh her by seventy pounds. Handing over the turkey at this point would be pretty tacky. "I think I can manage.''

She ducked her head. "Of course you can. You're being really nice and I appreciate it.'' She unlocked the door and held it open for him. "I'm guessing you know the way.''

Her place was the reverse of his, he noticed as he moved inside. A small area of linoleum led to a square living room. While his was on the left, hers was on the right. Which meant her kitchen was in the opposite direction. He turned toward the dining room, passed through it and found himself in the middle of her kitchen. She opened the refrigerator door and motioned to a shelf containing nothing but an empty roasting pan.

He deposited the bird into the pan, then glanced down at the wet spot on the front of his sweats. She followed his gaze and groaned.

"Sorry. I didn't realize he was leaking." She reached for a dish towel, made to approach him, then stopped and handed him the cloth.

Mark found himself wishing she'd offered to clean him up herself. He pushed the thought away as soon as it formed. No way was he going to get involved with another woman. Certainly not a neighbor. Hadn't he learned his lesson?

He rubbed at the damp spot, then tossed the towel back to her. "How many are you planning to feed with that?"

She unzipped her jacket and hung it on the back of a light oak chair. Her kitchen table was white tile edged in oak, surrounded by four matching wood chairs. He noticed that while her kitchen was physically the mirror image of his, nothing about it looked the same. His battered cabinets were a shade of green somewhere between mold and avocado, while hers were white and looked freshly painted. A blue border print circled the walls just below the ceiling. Plants hung at the sides of the big window where lace curtains had been pulled back to let in the light. As their landlord was a hands-off kind of guy, Mark knew that Darcy had made the improvements herself.

Neither apartment had anything so modern as a dishwasher, which meant he mostly used paper and plastic, when he bothered to eat at home. Darcy had a metal dish drainer placed neatly by the sink. Several pots were stacked together, drying in the late afternoon.

He returned his attention to her only to realize she was avoiding his gaze. She shifted uncomfortably.

"There were supposed to be ten of us, including you," she muttered, studying the toes of her boots. "It's actually good news for Millie that she can't make it. Her husband—soon to be ex-husband—ran off with some young girl. Millie's been struggling ever since. Her folks invited her home for Thanksgiving. She's hoping they can reconcile and that her parents will ask her to move home. She's got three kids and desperately wants to finish her college degree so she can get a decent job. So it's all for the best."

He digested the information, wondering if he should ask who Millie was, then decided it didn't matter. "So how many will there be now?"

She glanced at him. "Six. Millie has three kids." She offered a bright smile. "I like having a lot of people around for the holidays. I try to find people like you—with nowhere to go, no family around. As I said before, it's a tough time to be alone."

Great. A table full of strays.

She tucked a loose strand of hair behind her ear. The movement drew his attention to her soft-looking blond curls and the way her sweater outlined a sweet pair of full breasts. He might have spent the past few months recovering from a couple of bullet wounds, but parts of him had never been injured. They chose that moment to remind him that a man had needs.

Blood flowed south with a speed and intensity that made him grit his teeth. Damn. Why did he have to notice Darcy was attractive? He'd managed to avoid that particular truth for the past couple of months they'd been neighbors.

"Where's *your* family?" he asked, determined to ignore the pressure from his body. He willed away his desire.

"My folks died five years ago."

He didn't say anything. His parents had died, as well, but he wasn't about to bond with her over the fact. He didn't want anything in common with her. Was it just him, or was it hot in here?

"Can I get you something?" Darcy asked. "Tea? Cookies?"

"Made with whole-wheat flour and tofu? No thanks."

She laughed. "While I *do* make the cookies myself, I promise I use very normal ingredients."

"You probably consider tofu normal."

"Not when I bake. Although I've used carob before, if that counts."

He couldn't begin to imagine what carob was. "I need to be getting back."

She followed him to the door. "Thanks for helping me, Mark. I'm sure I could have wrestled Mr. Turkey inside myself but it was nice not have to mess with him."

The top of her head didn't even clear his shoulders. She looked innocent and wholesome. He had no business being here.

"Look, Darcy…"

He paused, not sure how to tell her he wouldn't make it for Thanksgiving dinner. He wasn't very social these days and he couldn't imagine anything more torturous than eating with five people he didn't know and didn't want to know.

Her blue eyes stared at him, while the corners of her full mouth turned up slightly. She had perfect skin. Clear, pale and nearly luminous. But the worst of it was the complete trust in her eyes. He had a bad feeling that she'd never told a white lie, let alone a really soul-threatening one. He felt as if he was about to kick a puppy.

His shoulders slumped. "Do you want me to bring anything for Thursday? Like wine?"

"Wine would be nice. I know absolutely nothing about it."

He nodded and left without looking at her. He didn't want to see her smiling at him as though he'd just done something amazing.

After he entered his own apartment, he stretched his cooling muscles, then headed down the tiny hall. Once in his bathroom, he tugged off his T-shirt and the thermal shirt underneath. Bare chested, he stared into the mirror.

The scar from the bullet wound in his side was still red and thick. He probed at it, remembering how the doctors had told him he'd been lucky. A few millimeters toward the center and he would have lost a major organ or two. Sylvia had been aiming for his heart. As it was, he'd nearly bled to death. He bent down to massage his leg. That bullet wound didn't give him nearly as much trouble as it had even a month ago.

When he'd been in the hospital, a lot of the guys from the precinct had come by to visit, most of them teasing him that bullet scars were a chick magnet. Somehow he couldn't see a woman like Darcy cooing over his injuries. She'd probably take one look and pass out. Not that he planned on showing her anything.

He straightened and turned on the water, then pulled off the rest of his clothes. As he stepped into the steaming shower, he reminded himself that, however much he found Darcy attractive, he wasn't about to go there. As he'd already learned the hard way, getting involved with a woman could be fatal.

Chapter Two

The great room at the Madison School was nearly forty feet square, with a huge rock fireplace in one wall. Half a dozen sofas formed conversation groups, while card tables set up around the perimeter of the room offered places to play different games. The high-beamed ceiling added to the open feel of the space. The smell of wood smoke mingled with the lingering scent of popcorn from last night's snack.

Darcy sat on a sofa in the corner, her feet tucked under her, listening intently as her brother, Dirk, described everything he'd packed in his suitcase.

"I even remembered my brush and comb," he said proudly.

Darcy's heart swelled with love for him as she studied his familiar face. They both had blue eyes and blond hair, but Dirk's features were more masculine.

And as much as it tweaked her ego, she had to admit he was the better looking of the siblings. At fourteen, he should have been suffering from skin troubles and a cracking voice. Instead he appeared to be making the transition into adolescence and manhood with little pain. He was growing steadily, which kept him lean, his skin was clear and she noticed the faint hint of a beard on his chin. Her baby brother was growing up.

"I'm impressed with your packing skills," she said sincerely. "I have never taken a trip without forgetting something. Remember, when I went off to college and left all my registration stuff at home?"

Dirk laughed. "Mom had to bring it to you and she got real mad. You were in trouble on your first day."

Darcy smiled at the memory, even as she tried to remember what it had felt like to be so irresponsible. Life had been easy back then—the world had been at her beck and call. Not anymore.

"You're rarely in trouble," she said.

Dirk beamed. "I can remember all the rules. Some of them are dumb, but I follow them. I like it here, Darcy. I want to stay."

"I know." She leaned forward and took his hand in hers. "You *will* stay right up until you're ready to be on your own."

He looked doubtful at the prospect. Darcy didn't blame him. Self-sufficiency was years away for him, but the Madison School was one of the best in the country. The well-trained staff specialized in helping developmentally disabled teens become happy, productive adults. The process could take years, but

Darcy was prepared to be patient. All the reports so far had been positive. Besides, Dirk was worth it.

"In the meantime," she continued, "I guess you're going to travel the world, aren't you?"

He grinned. "I'm not going to see the world. Just Chicago."

He made it sound like no big deal, but she saw the excitement brightening his eyes.

"Andrew says it's cold there, so I'm taking my warmest jacket," he continued. "You bought it for me last month. Remember?"

Darcy nodded.

"We're going to sleep on the train. Andrew says the hotel will have a Turkey dinner for us when we get there."

"I want to hear all about it," Darcy said. "Will you write in your journal so you can remember everything?"

He nodded. "I have the camera you gave me for my birthday. I'm going to take lots of pictures."

"Oh. That reminds me." Darcy bent down and fished through her purse. She pulled out a three-pack of film for his camera. "This is for you."

Dirk looked at the gift, then at her. "Darcy?"

She knew what he was asking—what worry drew his brows together and made him study her so carefully. Her brother might have the slow, studied air of someone out of step with the mainstream world, but he wasn't an idiot. He knew that money had been tight for them for a long time. While he didn't know what the school cost her or how many nights she stared into the darkness and prayed she would be able to hold it all together, he guessed that life still wasn't easy for her.

She gave him a quick hug. "It's just film, Dirk. I can afford it."

He still looked worried when she released him. "I have my allowance. I can pay you back."

"No. That's *your* money. Spend it on something for you. Oh, but if you want to bring me back a postcard from Chicago, I wouldn't say no."

He nodded. "I'll bring you two."

"That would be great."

He took the film she offered and turned the boxes over in his hands. In his chambray shirt and worn jeans, he looked like any other fourteen-year-old. But he wasn't. His difficulties had become apparent within the first year of his life. Darcy's parents had despaired, but Dirk's uniqueness had only made her love him more.

"I'm going to miss you tomorrow," she said, changing the subject. "I'll be thinking about you."

It was the first Thanksgiving they'd been apart. She tried not to mind.

Happiness poured back into his eyes. "We're going on the train. I've never been on the train." His smile faded. "I'll miss you, too, Darcy."

"Hey, no long faces. Only happy people get to go to Chicago."

Both Darcy and Dirk glanced up as Andrew, one of the counselors at the school, joined them. He settled on the wing chair next to the sofa.

"How are you doing, Darcy? Keeping busy?"

She thought of her shift at the Hip Hop, followed

by hours of baking every afternoon and evening. She had to shop for supplies for her home business and find time to make deliveries. Then there was the small matter of preparing a Thanksgiving dinner on a rare day off.

"I manage to keep myself occupied," she said ruefully.

"I know you do." He turned toward Dirk and nodded at the film still in his hands. "You're going to see a lot of really great things in the city. Darcy's going to be excited about your pictures."

Dirk grinned. "I'll put them in my photo album and write down what they were."

"I look forward to that," Darcy said honestly. She wanted to hear every detail of her brother's first trip without her.

"He's been getting really good with his photography," Andrew said. "He's got several of the other students interested as well. After the first of the year, a local photographer is going to be teaching a class a couple of times a week."

"That sounds fabulous."

"We do whatever works," he said.

Darcy leaned back against the sofa and let the warmth of contentment flow over her. Whenever she questioned her decision to uproot Dirk and herself and move to Montana of all places, she reminded herself that this school was one of the best in the country. Where else would her brother get full-time attention from an excellent staff? Andrew, a Ph.D. in his mid-thirties, lived in the facility with his wife, who was expecting their first child. Most of the staff lived on the extensive grounds in private homes. Experts in various fields were brought in to teach the students. Activities were kept interesting and practical.

The trip to Chicago was one example. The students would have the experience of riding on a train, staying in a hotel and exploring a large city all under the careful supervision of the staff. The school offered two or three such trips each year. By the time Dirk was ready to be on his own, he would know what it was like to travel by train or plane, rent a room, order in a restaurant, go to a museum, ask for directions and find his way home. These were experiences she couldn't begin to give him.

"Dirk's doing well," Andrew said, giving the boy a thumbs-up. "He's made a lot of friends."

Yet another thing she couldn't give him, she thought happily. The opportunity to interact with peers.

"I'm glad," she said.

Andrew rose. "Stop by my office on your way out. I'll show you Dirk's progress report."

"I'll do that."

He winked at them and left.

Darcy patted her brother's arm. "I'm so glad you're happy here. This is a good school."

"I'm learning a lot," he said. "I try real hard, Darcy. When we go to the grocery store, I can give the lady the right amount and sometimes I even know the change." He wrinkled his nose. "But I don't understand fractions. They're really hard."

She laughed. "You know what? I don't get them, either, so it's not just you."

He took her hand. "What will you do tomorrow on Thanksgiving?"

"I'll miss you." She squeezed his fingers. "And I'll cook a turkey."

"Is it big?"

"Twenty-four pounds. Maybe next week I'll make up a dish of enchiladas and bring them when I visit you."

"I'd like that." He leaned close. "Who will be at dinner tomorrow?"

Oh, there was a subject she wasn't excited about. "The party is shrinking," she complained, trying to ignore the sense of panic inside. "My friend Millie and her children won't be there. They're going home to spend the holiday with her family. And another couple has decided they would rather be alone." Now it was just two other people, plus Mark. She'd been hoping for more of a crowd. "My next-door neighbor is coming. His name is Mark and he works for the sheriff's office."

Dirk looked impressed. "Is he nice?"

"He's quiet," she said, not sure she would ever use the word "nice" to describe Mark Kincaid. "He used to live in New York City. He was a detective."

Dirk frowned. "He must know a lot of bad people. I wouldn't like that."

"Me, either."

Someone at a nearby table called for her and Dirk to join them to play a game. Darcy stayed long enough to eat dinner with her brother and to admire his tidy packing job. She left shortly before eight, promising to come back after his trip so she could hear about everything.

On the drive home to Whitehorn, she played the radio and tried not to think about the following day. She was foolishly nervous at the thought of spending a couple of hours in the presence of Mark Kincaid. If only Dirk was going to be there. Not only would she enjoy spending the time with her brother, he would be a perfect buffer between herself and Mark. Of course, if Mark came to Thanksgiving while her brother was in residence, she wouldn't *have* a Mark Kincaid problem. In the past five years she hadn't met a single man who hadn't turned tail and run when he'd found out that she was Dirk's only relative, and therefore physically and financially responsible for him.

So there was no point in getting all hot and bothered about her new neighbor. They didn't have a relationship and they weren't going to have one. This, despite her attraction to the man. Besides, it wasn't as if she even remembered how to do the whole man-woman thing.

The dark highway stretched out in front of her. Past the light of her headlights, she saw nothing but a few stars glittering in the sky. Tonight the emptiness made her feel sad and lonely. Most of the time she was able to keep busy enough not to notice that she didn't have any close friends, let alone romantic entanglements.

It would be nice to have an understanding with someone who cared about her romantically. Or even sexually. Sometimes her body ached with longing. She hadn't been on a real date in five years. Not that

tomorrow was a date. She'd invited her neighbor over
for Thanksgiving dinner. The event didn't have any
emotional significance. If she thought it did, she was
only fooling herself.

Unable to think of an excuse not to come, Mark
rang Darcy's doorbell promptly at four. He'd checked
his pager three times that day to make sure it was
working. Unfortunately, no crime spree had occurred
in the sleepy town of Whitehorn and he hadn't been
called in to work. So here he was, carrying a bottle
of wine and a bouquet of flowers. He felt like an idiot.

Darcy opened the door. Her hair was its usual dis-
array of curls. Color stained her cheeks and she
started babbling the second she saw him.

"I'm so sorry, Mark. I didn't plan this, but I don't
know that you're going to believe me. It's just one
of those things. Who could have guessed that the Wil-
sons would rather spend the day alone? Like she can
even cook. Oh, but I don't mean that in a bad way. I
mean I like her and all, it's just they're not here. And
I already told you about Millie and her kids. Then
Margaret ended up getting called in to work. I mean
she's a nurse, so what could she say but yes, and
Betty got a cold and feels awful. Plus she didn't want
to spread around her germs. So I couldn't exactly
force any of them, could I?"

She looked both chagrined and cautiously hopeful.
Mark shivered. He'd crossed the distance between the
two apartments without bothering to pull on a coat.
He wore slacks and a long sleeved shirt and the temperature outside couldn't be above twenty.

"I don't know what you're talking about," he said, "but could we straighten it out inside?"

"What?" She stared at him. "Oh! You must be freezing. Come on in."

She held the door open wide, then took the wine and flowers he offered. She gazed at the yellow roses and orange Gerber daises as if she'd never seen them before.

"You brought me flowers," she murmured, inhaling the scent of the blooms. "Wow. That's so nice." She stared at him as if he'd just created fire. "I mean really nice."

He bit back a statement that he wasn't the least bit nice. "I thought maybe for the table."

"Of course. They're perfect."

She led the way into the dining room. He noticed the large table had only two place settings. Her incoherent conversation replayed in his brain.

"No one else will be here for dinner?" he asked.

She shook her head as she reached for a vase in the hutch against the far wall. "No. Sorry. I didn't plan this. I hope you believe me."

She glanced over her shoulder as if expecting him to explode with rage. Mark thought about the alternative to eating dinner with just Darcy and that was eating dinner with her and half a dozen people he didn't know. People who would want to ask questions.

"I'm not a real social guy. It doesn't matter."

She set the wine on the table, then clutched the flowers and the vase to her chest. "Really? I didn't want you to think I'd set this up on purpose."

Her meaning was slow to sink in. Set up as in… synapses fired in his brain. As in a date.

His gaze settled on her as he took in her appearance. Instead of her usual waitress uniform, she wore a bright blue sweater and black slacks. Both emphasized her curves. She might not be tall, but she had all the right parts in the perfect proportions. He avoided staring at her breasts because they'd gotten him into trouble the last time he'd been in her house. Of course, admiring her legs wasn't much safer. Maybe he should keep his attention on her face.

"I promise not to think the worst of you without more evidence," he said seriously.

She grinned. "Good. Then would you mind opening the wine? Oh, and I hope you're hungry, because I expect you to eat your half of the turkey."

"You first."

He grabbed the wine and followed her into the kitchen. The scent of cooking turkey mingled with other smells. There were three pots bubbling on the stove and the microwave beeped impatiently.

"Glasses are in there," she said, pointing to a cupboard by the tile and oak table.

She turned her attention to the stove, lifting covers and stirring, all the while muttering under her breath. He didn't know if she was talking to herself or the food, then decided it didn't matter. Women in the kitchen were a mystery he'd never solved. They moved with an easy grace he could never imagine duplicating. Perhaps because he hadn't seen it a great deal while growing up. His mother had never been much for cooking, and his sister was too busy being queen of the rodeo to bother with meal preparation.

"It all smells good," he said as he poured the wine.

She took the glass he offered and leaned against the counter. "I'm not expecting a crisis." Laughter brightened her eyes. "That's not to say I haven't had them in the past, before I knew what I was doing. However I've learned from my mistakes."

He put the open bottle on the counter. "What kind of mistakes."

"Oh, little things like not realizing that a turkey takes several days to thaw. That was before I special-ordered a fresh one. So I tried cooking it while still frozen." She winced. "Which meant it took hours and all that nasty stuff they put on the inside like the neck and heart cooked with it. You wouldn't believe the smell. We had to go out that Thanksgiving. And let me tell you, there's not a whole lot open. Then there was the time I was really in a hurry and accidentally put salt in to thicken the gravy instead of flour. There were some gagging sounds around the table that night!"

"When did you start cooking?"

"About five years ago."

"What inspired you?"

"We all have to grow up some time." She shrugged. "Five years ago, I doubt I could have boiled water without instructions. Since then I've read and practiced. Working in restaurants allowed me to observe different techniques. I found out I really like baking." She motioned to the pies cooling on the table. "I made those myself, this morning."

There were three pies, including one pumpkin. "Do I have to eat half of those, too?"

"Maybe. We'll see how you do on the turkey." She put her wine on the counter and returned her attention to the stove. "I've started selling my baked goods around town. I might have a shot at a contract with the Hip Hop Café. They're handing out samples to see if people like my stuff."

"So that was *your* pumpkin bread I tried on Monday."

"Yes. And you liked it. Even though you make such a fuss about eating vegetables at breakfast."

"It's not natural."

"Do we have to have the omelette conversation again?"

"Not if you don't want to."

She opened the oven and poked at the turkey. "He's nearly ready." When she closed the door, she straightened. "You'll be pleased to know there's nothing unnatural about our meal this evening."

"I was afraid of that."

"Why?"

"You're into health foods. I'm nervous about your choice of ingredients."

She laughed. "Tofu surprise in the stuffing?"

"Exactly."

She planted her hands on her hips. "What is it about men and tofu. You're all deathly afraid women are plotting to get you to eat it."

"Aren't you?"

"Maybe," she admitted.

Mark found himself chuckling. The action felt awkward and unfamiliar. He'd worried about spending time with Darcy, but she was surprisingly easy to be with. And easy on the eye. When she returned her attention to the stove, he found his gaze lingering on the curve of her rear. He reminded himself that attraction was dangerous. Life was better when he didn't feel anything. How many times did he have to get shot before he learned his lesson?

"Is it snowing?" she asked.

"Not yet, but it was pretty gray this afternoon. It's supposed to snow tonight."

"Good. I like holidays with snow. Oh. Isn't there a football game on this afternoon. Do you want to go watch it?"

"Contrary to popular opinion, I *am* capable of going an entire day without viewing a sporting event."

She looked at him in mock amazement. "Really? How do you do it? Deep breathing exercises?"

"Tremendous willpower."

"I'm very impressed." She carried a pot over to the sink and drained it. "While you're not watching football, would you mind taking our little friend out of the oven. He should be done."

Mark set down his wine, then carried the turkey over to the table. Darcy wrapped the bird in foil, explaining that it had to rest before carving. He didn't think it had been especially active before now, but what did he know about turkey cooking?

She had him mash the potatoes while she made the gravy—since when did gravy *not* come out of a can—then she expertly carved several slices from the impressive bird and quickly put all the dishes on the table.

They sat across from each other. Mark had a moment of awkwardness—the situation was too intimate for his liking. Instinctively he went into detective mode, finding safety in asking questions.

"How long have you lived in Whitehorn?" he asked as she passed him the platter of turkey.

"Since early June," she said. "Before that I lived in Arizona for a few years and before that, Chicago."

"Is that where you're from?"

"Yes. I grew up in a wealthy suburb you've probably never heard of, where my most complex decision was which invitation to accept to the prom. The boy's coolness was, of course, the deciding factor."

She was teasing but also telling the truth, he thought. Funny, she didn't look like the idle princess type. "You were one of the popular girls?"

"Even a cheerleader. I wince at the memory of my shallow existence." She passed him a green bean casserole, followed by a dish of yams. "I went off to college without a clue as to what I wanted to be when I grew up. Of course, I don't think I actually wanted to be an adult. I kept switching majors and playing rather than studying. I nearly accepted a marriage proposal rather than choose a direction for my studies."

Her blue eyes darkened with the memories. "Not my finest hour."

He had a hard time reconciling her story with the woman in front of him. "What happened?"

She took a bite of turkey and chewed. When she'd swallowed, she said, "My parents died in a car crash.

I was unprepared, to say the least.'' She hesitated, as if there was more she was going to say.

Mark waited. The detective in him wanted to push for information, but he reminded himself that he was a guest in her home and it was a holiday.

"This is really good," he said when he'd tasted the turkey.

"Thanks."

"How old were you when your parents died?"

"Twenty, but ignorant, if you know what I mean. In addition to dealing with the shock of losing them at once, I had the horror of getting calls from their attorney, who wanted to explain things to me."

She sighed softly at the memory. "My parents left a pile of bills. Apparently they'd been separated for a couple of years but hadn't wanted me to know. My dad had a penthouse in the city, we all had new cars. By the time everything was paid off, there wasn't much left. I had to drop out of school." She stabbed at her mashed potatoes.

"The sad part is, I could have handled the news of their pending divorce if they'd bothered to tell me. At least we could have had an honest conversation before they died. Plus it turned out most of my friends were more interested in my lack of social standing and financial resources than in staying loyal. I grew up fast. By the time the dust settled, I was ready to take care of myself."

She had an open face, he thought, watching her. Every emotion flashed across her eyes. She would be a lousy poker player.

"You seem to have done a good job," he said.

"Thanks. I tried."

He touched the dining room table. "This looks old. Is it a family antique you managed to salvage?"

She laughed. "I'm sure it's someone's but not mine. I bought it a couple of years ago at a garage sale. The hutch came with it." She grinned. "These days, I live for a good bargain. You should see me at the half-yearly sales. I'm formidable."

"Sounds like it. Do you miss being rich?"

"Who wouldn't?" She scooped up a forkful of stuffing. "But I like who I am now a whole lot more than I liked who I was before. I consider that a plus."

She was a pint-size bundle of trouble, he thought grimly. Pretty, sexy, single and appealing. Why had he ever accepted her invitation?

"What brings you to Whitehorn?" he asked. "It's a long way from Arizona."

For the first time that evening, she avoided his gaze. "I wanted to experience 'big sky country,'" she said breezily. "You know—the myth of the Old West. I just sort of found my way here."

Mark's chest tightened. She was lying. He would bet his life on it. Which meant there was something she didn't want him to know. Like Sylvia, she was a woman with secrets—and off-limits to him.

Chapter Three

After dinner, they cleared the table, then Darcy led the way into the small living room. Mark followed, sitting at the opposite end of the sofa.

"That was great," he said. "I'm impressed."

"Thank you." She patted her stomach. "I'm full but don't feel as if I'm about to explode. I consider that a positive statement after a Thanksgiving dinner."

"I didn't get through my half of the turkey."

She laughed. "That's right. You were supposed to eat your whole twelve pounds' worth. Maybe I should pack it up and you can take it home. I have a great recipe for turkey enchiladas. I could write it down for you."

"I don't cook much."

She pretended surprise. "I thought all New York City detectives were incredibly domestic."

"I missed that class." He studied her. "So you know I lived in New York. Am I a regular topic for gossip or is it just a sometime thing?"

Darcy refused to give in to the embarrassment she could feel growing inside her. "Everyone has his or her fifteen minutes of fame at the Hip Hop Café," she said casually. "You were a hot topic when you moved back, but things have calmed down some since then."

"Good to know."

Darcy sipped her wine and regarded her guest over the rim of her glass. He was a good-looking man. Too good-looking for her long-celibate state. Tall, strong, with compelling green eyes. She liked that his dark brown hair was a tad too long and that his tailored slacks showed off his perfect butt nearly as much as his jeans did.

She took another quick sip to keep herself from grinning. She couldn't believe she was sitting here thinking about Mark's butt. She had no right—nor was it her style. Even back in the dark ages when she'd actually dated, she'd never been overly interested in sex. She'd given in because it had been expected, but most of the time, she'd been faintly bored by the experience. In the past five years she'd missed the emotional closeness of male-female relationships more than the physical intimacy...right up until she'd laid eyes on Mark.

Something about the man set her body to humming. She sort of enjoyed the sensation of being faintly aroused without him actually doing anything. At least it was a change from her usual worry and exhaustion.

He'd surprised her by being a pleasant guest. She'd thought he might not talk at all, which had made the thought of just the two of them at the table fairly horrifying. For a few minutes he'd seemed to withdraw into himself, but he'd recovered and had continued with his questions. Speaking of which...

"I think it's my turn to play detective," she said teasingly. "You learned everything about me at dinner, so now I should learn about you."

"Ask away."

She shifted so that she was facing him. "How did a man born and bred in Montana end up in New York? As a detective, no less?"

"It's something I wanted from the time I was a kid. I never got the rodeo bug, so I wasn't interested in steer wrestling or bronc riding. I spent my time reading police procedurals. When I graduated from college, I headed for New York where I got a job on the police force. I worked my way up from there."

His expression didn't change as he spoke and Darcy had a difficult time figuring out if the memories made him sad.

"What brought you back?" she asked.

"I was shot."

She nearly spilled her wine. "In the line of duty?"

"A murder suspect didn't like the way the investigation was going. She took out her temper on me."

Darcy stared at him in shock. "She? A woman shot you?"

"Women can be killers, too."

"I suppose." She studied him, looking for healing scars or hints that he'd been hurt. There weren't any—nothing was visible and he didn't walk with a limp. She'd seen him out jogging so he must be doing better. She thought about asking where he'd been wounded, but the question felt too intimate. "I don't think of the average woman as being a violent person."

"She isn't. But there are always exceptions."

"Do you miss the work?"

He shifted uncomfortably, as if he didn't want to answer the question. "Some."

"Do you miss the city?"

"It sure ain't Whitehorn."

She laughed. "You have that right. I remember growing up in Chicago. We were always going into the city on weekends to different restaurants and plays. Or to the museums."

"There's a great western museum not too far from here."

"Gee, thanks. Next you'll be telling me that the Hip Hop Café serves international cuisine."

"They do offer an Oriental chicken salad on the menu."

She took another sip of wine. "I actually knew that."

He picked up his glass from the coffee table. "Okay, so Whitehorn doesn't exactly have the same amenities. I'll admit I do miss New York. The ethnic foods were great, as was the idea that I could get anything I wanted at any time of the day or night. Detective work isn't nine-to-five, so we appreciated the late hours the restaurants were open." He drank from his glass. "I was never much of a museum guy, but I did enjoy theater." He frowned slightly. "I don't think I ever saw the end of a play. I nearly always got called to a crime scene."

She leaned her head against the sofa back. "I can't begin to relate to your experiences."

"I wouldn't want you to. Sometimes they make it hard to sleep at night."

She waited, but he didn't say more. Did he have trouble sleeping? Did he pace long into the night? Lamplight highlighted the strength of his jaw. He had a well-shaped mouth, she thought dreamily. She would bet ten bucks that Detective Mark Kincaid was one fine kisser. Not that she was going to find out, but a girl could dream. She smiled at the thought of telling him kissing might make sleeping easier...or not.

"You're not married," she said before she could stop herself.

His eyebrows rose slightly. "No. Never have been."

"Me, either."

"No surprise there. You're barely old enough to be legal."

"I'm twenty-five."

"A baby."

She straightened. "You're hardly in your dotage."

"It's not the miles, it's the wear and tear."

He smiled as he spoke. A teasing curve of lips that made her heart stutter against her ribs and her hands suddenly go damp. She had to be extra careful when she put down her glass so that it didn't slip.

"You should smile more," she said.

His good humor faded. "I don't find life especially funny."

"Maybe not, but there are still pleasant surprises. Tonight, for example. I was worried and nervous about you coming over to dinner, but it's turned out fine. We've chatted more easily than I would have thought."

"I'll give you that," he said. "I didn't want to come. The way you badger me about what I eat, I was sure you were going to put tofu in something."

"You didn't even taste it."

His eyes widened. "Darcy."

He growled her name more than said it. Shivers trickled down her spine. She found herself wanting to lean toward him, press against him to see what would happen. Dangerous thoughts, she told herself. She must make sure to keep them to herself.

"It was in the mashed potatoes," she whispered. "I would never put tofu in the stuffing."

He laughed. She'd never heard him laugh before— not that they'd spent all that much time together. Most of their conversations had been abbreviated exchanges with her arguing about his breakfast choice.

"I'll bet you don't even have tofu in the house," he said, then finished his wine.

"You're right, but I will admit to the pleasure of watching a grown man tremble at the thought." She rose and stretched. "There's probably one more glass of wine in the bottle,'' she said. ''As you're not driving, why don't you finish it?''

He nodded his agreement and she walked into the dining room. The wine bottle stood on the table. She grabbed it. As she approached the sofa, she fought against the urge to slide down next to him. What would the detective say if she suddenly plopped herself down close, maybe even *on* his lap. She giggled as she pictured him leaping up in horror. The wine would spill on her sofa and she would be humiliated. It was probably best if she kept her feelings to herself.

''What's so funny?'' he asked.

''Just my own twisted sense of humor.''

He held out his glass. She bent toward him to pour, but instead of focusing on what she was doing, she found herself staring into his green eyes. She didn't think she'd ever known a man with green eyes before. They were actually beautiful—well shaped and fringed with long, dark lashes.

''Darcy?''

She heard him speak her name, but she couldn't respond. Her heart thundered painfully in her chest. There was a pressure, as well, as if all the air had been sucked out of the room. She felt unbearably warm, yet her legs were trembling. If not from cold, then from what?

Mark took the wine bottle from her. She glanced down and saw she hadn't poured any of the pale liquid. He set his glass on the table, next to the bottle, all the while keeping his gaze firmly locked with hers.

''We can't do this,'' he said.

She licked her suddenly dry lips. ''Do what?''

He swore. She realized she was still bent over him. Like an idiot, she thought, starting to straighten. But then his hand was on her arm, tugging her closer. She didn't know which way to move. Her center of balance shifted and suddenly she was falling.

Before she could stop herself, she landed on his lap—exactly where she'd imagined herself not thirty seconds before. His arms came around her, drawing her closer.

"You're not the only one who's been thinking about it," he said quietly, right before his mouth settled over hers.

For several seconds Darcy couldn't respond. She was afraid she was imagining all this. That the wine had gone to her head—so much so that on another plane of reality, she and Mark were actually having a rational conversation while her imagination created this romantic scenario.

Yet he felt very real as he pulled her against him. She wasn't sure her fantasizing could have created such an amazing combination of heat and desire.

As she'd thought, Mark Kincaid kissed like a dream. Soft yet firm, warm and tempting. He didn't take, didn't hold back, didn't give her time to think, which was all exactly how she wanted it. His lips brushed against hers in a sensual greeting that made her toes curl. His scent, the feel of his body against hers, the way his arms wrapped around her, pulling her against him were all delightfully unfamiliar, but oh, so welcome.

He kept the kiss light, yet despite the delicate pressure, she found herself overwhelmed by need. Heat poured through her with an intensity she'd never experienced. She knew however unexpected the turn of events, they were very real.

Every cell in her body cried out for her to have her way with this man. She tried to tell herself that she had to be careful not to scare him off, that she needed to be the tiniest bit sensible and that it had been at least five years since she'd been with a man and she'd probably forgotten how to do it. None of that mattered. Not when his mouth moved over hers, back and forth, slowly, so slowly.

He tilted his head to improve the angle of their contact. Instinctively she parted for him, wanting him to kiss her deeply, needing that intimacy more than she'd ever needed anything. But he made her wait. First he nibbled on her lower lip, the pull of his teeth nearly making her cry out with pleasure. Her breasts swelled and began to ache. Without meaning to, she found herself moving her hands up his shoulders to his neck, then burying her fingers in his hair.

Finally, amazingly, he swept his tongue against the inside of her lower lip. Desire shot through her, making her cling to him. Something hard and masculine bumped up against her hip. The proof of his arousal made her brush her tongue against his, taking rather than waiting.

It was as if she'd set fire to dynamite. Passion exploded through her. Through Mark, as well, if his actions told the truth. Even as they leaned into each other, trying to kiss more deeply, to explore every aspect of their sensual connection, their hands reached for each other.

He grabbed her hips, lifting her. She shifted around until she straddled him. Instantly her hot, ready feminine center pressed against his hardness. The perfect pleasure of the contact nearly made her scream. She couldn't stop the pulsating movement of her hips, or the catch in her breath when she found a rhythm that nearly sent her over the edge. Mark only made it worse—and better—by urging her on. The hands holding her hips eased her back and forth until they both moaned.

He pulled away enough to kiss her cheeks, her chin, then to nibble along her throat. He moved his hands from her hips to her waist, then around to her ribs. From there it was a short journey to her breasts.

She was too stunned to protest...at least that's what she tried telling herself in the tiny part of her brain that was still coherent. This wasn't her fault. Except she'd *wanted* it to happen, had imagined what it would be like. Instead of stopping him, she arched her back, pushing her full curves into his hands. He squeezed gently, then explored her. When his fingers brushed against her nipples, she cried out, exhaling his name.

When he tugged on the hem of her sweater, she helped him pull off the garment. He unfastened her bra without a single fumble, leaving her bare to the waist. Before she could even think about being embarrassed or stopping him, he straightened and leaned forward, then took her right nipple in his mouth.

The sensation was nearly more than she could stand. As his lips closed around her and his tongue flicked against her taut peak, he used his fingers to tease her other breast. She clutched at him, feeling the silk of his hair. Powerful muscles bunched as he shuddered.

The voice whispering *this had to stop* began to fade as desire pulsed in time with her rapid heartbeat. Tears burned in her eyes—brought on by skin long deprived of human touch. Every brush of his fingers was exquisite. When he stood her on her feet and reached for the button at her waistband, she didn't have the will to stop him. Especially when his fingers trembled slightly. She looked at his face. The raw need in his green eyes reassured her more than words.

He unfastened her slacks. Before tugging them down, he paused to shrug out of his shirt. She had a brief impression of strong muscles and a still-red scar, but then he urged her out of her shoes and she couldn't think about anything except him pulling off the rest of her clothes.

He settled back on the sofa, then ran his hands up and down her legs, pausing at the top of her thighs. The pulsing desire had only increased and when he swept close to the blond hair protecting her most private place, she began to quiver. He wrapped his arms around her waist and pulled her down next to him on the cushion. They kissed. A deep, stirring sharing of souls that made her shake even more.

Long fingers rested on her thigh. She parted slightly, so ready she knew that it wouldn't take but a touch to bring her to climax.

"Mark, I—"

He touched her there. Through the slick folds of skin, the dampness, he found the one spot designed to bring her to her knees. She couldn't speak, couldn't breathe, couldn't do anything but silently beg him to never stop.

He read her mind.

With agonizing slowness, he circled the sensitive place, then returned to brush over the swollen nerve center. Twice more he repeated the process and, on the third lap, she lost herself.

Her climax shuddered through her with the intensity of a volcano. He deepened the kiss, swallowing her cries as pleasure rippled through her, making her shake and cling to him. He touched her lightly until the last tremor faded.

He drew back slightly and stroked her cheek. When she finally gathered the courage to open her eyes, she found him smiling at her. The slow, easy, masculine smile of a man who has just pleased a woman.

"Yes, well." She cleared her throat. "It's been some time since I've, ah…"

"I hadn't noticed."

"Liar."

His smile widened. "All right. Maybe I noticed a little. It happened so quickly, it was hard to tell."

She swatted at his arm, but without any great force. He slipped off the sofa, then turned her so she was half sitting, half lying against the back. She tried not to think about the fact that she was completely naked and that they were in her living room. Not to mention that she barely knew the man. But when she would have protested, he bent down and nibbled the skin at the inside of her knee.

"Wh-what are you doing?" she asked breathlessly

because she already had a good idea of where he was heading.

"If it's been a long time, you probably need a little more excitement in your life. If you don't like this, just tell me to stop."

Yeah right, she thought hazily as the nibbling moved up higher. She parted her legs to make things easier for him and closed her eyes when he reached the inside of her thighs. So much for her not thinking sex was all that special. Obviously, until now, she'd been doing it wrong.

At the exact moment he gave her the most intimate kiss possible, he pressed his hand against her breast. The combination of sensations nearly made her scream. He teased her nipple in perfect counterpart to the movements of his tongue between her legs. All those needs returned, as if she hadn't just found her release. Pressure built with a speed that left her breathless.

More. She needed more. She brought her feet up to the sofa, parting her legs even wider. He licked her most sensitive place, tasting all of her. He removed his hand from her breast, but before she could protest, a single finger entered her. He slipped in and out slowly, then faster and faster, all the while kissing and licking and nibbling until she thought she might die from the glory of it all.

She clutched at the sofa cushions. Perspiration broke out on her body. Pressure built then released in an unexpected shudder that left her unable to hold back her cry of delight. It was more than she'd ever experienced, and seemed to go on forever. He touched her gently, drawing every possible shiver of wonder from her starving body.

When she was finally back on earth, she sighed with contentment. Then something thick and hard pressed against her. She shifted so that she could wrap her legs around him, drawing him in.

"Yes," she breathed, opening her eyes.

Passion tightened Mark's features. He pushed inside her, filling her until she gasped.

"I want you," he growled.

"Please."

Mark told himself this was a mistake, but it was a little late now. As he pushed into Darcy's tight body, he groaned. She felt too good—hot, slick, ready. If only she hadn't looked at him as if she'd never before seen a man she wanted. If only he hadn't noticed the swell of her breasts earlier that afternoon. If only she hadn't responded like a starving person enjoying her first meal in weeks.

Remember what happened last time, he told himself, as he continued to push inside her. But this was different, he argued silently. No, she was a woman with secrets. He knew better.

Damn. She pulled him close and kissed him. As their tongues circled and danced, he felt himself losing control. She kissed better than anyone he'd ever been with. It's just sex, he told himself as he slipped toward the edge.

"Mark," she breathed, then gasped.

He felt the shudder of her release. It was more than he could resist. With a gasp of his own, he went over the cliff and began his journey to paradise.

Chapter Four

Darcy didn't have the luxury of waiting until the morning after to feel like an idiot. No, she got to feel stupid the second Mark straightened, pulling out of her body. There she was, naked as the day she was born, half sitting, half lying on her sofa while a strange man pulled up his trousers and zipped them. He hadn't even taken off his clothes.

Color flooded her face. She wanted to run and hide, but there was no easy way to extricate herself from the sofa. Plus there was the whole naked thing.

Frantically she looked around for something with which to cover herself. The sofa didn't offer many ideas. Mark must have noticed her distress, because he picked up his shirt and draped it over her, then rose to his feet. Something very like chagrin darkened his green eyes.

"Darcy, I—" He broke off and rubbed the back of his neck. "I don't do this sort of thing enough to know what to say."

"Me, either," she said, pulling on the shirt and buttoning it. She assumed they were discussing the suddenness of the encounter, and not the fact that they'd made love. Somehow Mark didn't strike her as sexually inexperienced. Could the situation be more awkward?

"I don't usually...that is I've never—" She pressed her lips together and wished she could simply fade into the fabric of the sofa.

He crouched in front of her and brushed the hair from her eyes. "I know. This isn't your style. Mine either. I guess we were both caught up in the moment." One corner of his mouth quirked up slightly. "Must have been all the tofu in the potatoes."

"Must have been."

He dropped his hand to his side. "Are you okay?" No!

She held in the word. "I'm not upset, well, not that much. It's just, I don't know. Too weird, I guess. I barely know you. We're not even dating." She swallowed and wanted to die. "Not that I'm hinting we *should* date, it's just..."

She looked away, hating what he must think of her. That she was cheap and easy. She wasn't—she'd never been that way. If she tried to explain about her life, he might start to ask questions and what was she supposed to say about Dirk? Talking about her brother was hardly post-lovemaking material.

He stood, then bent over and grabbed her clothes.

Darcy took them gratefully. She pulled on her panties, then rose and quickly pulled on her slacks. There was a really awkward moment when she had to hand him back his shirt, then slip on her bra and sweater all while trying to keep from thinking about him watching her. Which was crazy. The man had just touched about every significant body part she owned. Modesty was coming a little late to help.

When she was dressed, she forced herself to look at him. He stood with his hands shoved into his slacks pockets. Tension filled his body—a body that she had touched, that had entered hers. The memory of what they'd done to each other made her study the carpet again.

"I don't know what to say," she admitted.

"Do you want me to apologize?"

She stared at him and wished she knew what he was thinking. "Are you sorry?"

"No."

"Then don't apologize."

"Fair enough." He shifted his weight. "I'm guessing it's probably time for me to go."

She winced. "Of course." She headed for the door.

He followed her, then surprised her by bending down and kissing her cheek. "Thank you. That was an amazing experience."

"Um, yes well, for me, too." Despite her embarrassment and lingering horror at her impulsiveness, she couldn't complain about the physical aspects of their lovemaking. Mark had been amazing.

"I'll call you," he said.

"Don't say that." She forced herself to smile at him. "It's kind of a button for me. You don't have to call."

"What if I want to?"

"Then just do it, but don't tell me you're going to. If you do, I'll obsess about it and when you don't call, I'll try to figure out what I did wrong. Two weeks later I'll finally remember that it's not my problem, it's yours. But I don't need the emotional down time."

"There's nothing wrong with you," he said earnestly. "You're an incredibly attractive, sexy woman."

"As true as that may be, your gender can be stupid. So don't tell me you're going to call. Okay?"

"Deal."

He stared at her. She gazed into his green eyes, trying to memorize everything about him. Because she didn't have a doubt in her mind that except for incredibly stilted conversations at the diner, she wasn't going to see him again.

"Bye, Darcy. Thanks for the dinner."

She opened the door and he stepped into the night. She gave a quick wave as he hurried toward his own apartment. She got the door closed and was halfway to the kitchen when reality slammed into her with all the subtlety of a runaway dish tray hitting the floor.

She and Mark had just had sex. *Unprotected* sex.

Darcy leaned against the dining room wall. No. That couldn't have happened. She wasn't that stupid, was she? After five years of trying to get it right, she couldn't possibly have blown it. And for what? Thirty minutes of hot, wild, incredible sex? If she had a craving, couldn't she just stick to chocolate?

Still calling herself fifteen different kinds of moron, she crossed to the calendar and counted days. Okay, the pregnancy issue didn't seem to be a problem, but there were other considerations. For one thing, where exactly had Mark Kincaid been putting his handsome self? For another, even if her body got through this unscathed, what about her emotional well-being? One-night stands went against everything she believed in. She prided herself on being a thoughtful, intelligent, organized woman who made informed choices. She hadn't gotten through all the hell of the past few years by jumping into bed with every pretty face who asked.

Why had she allowed a juvenile crush on her good-looking neighbor to overwhelm her good sense? And what was she supposed to say to him the next time she saw him?

Darcy turned off the alarm two minutes before it was scheduled to go off. She stared at the time. Four fifty-eight. She figured she'd gotten maybe two hours of sleep the whole night. Worry and self-recrimination had kept her awake most of the time. When she had finally dozed off, she'd found herself dreaming about her close encounter with her sexy neighbor. The sensation of him kissing his way up her thighs had been enough to jerk her into consciousness.

Her eyes burned, her eyelids felt swollen and even

her hair hurt. She groaned as she forced herself into a sitting position. It was going to be a long day.

Cold water on her face and a vigorous teethbrushing didn't make her feel any better. Normally she waited until she was at the Hip Hop to have coffee, but this morning she needed an emergency infusion. Maybe a jolt of caffeine would jump-start her body. She pulled on her ratty terry-cloth robe and stumbled into the kitchen.

After flipping on lights and hunting up the coffeemaker, she dug out a filter and coffee, then set about making magic. She'd just turned on the machine when there was a soft tap at her back door.

Darcy froze. She knew she hadn't imagined the sound. She also had a really good idea of who would come calling at five in the morning, although she couldn't figure out why. Then she pictured herself— her hair sticking out at odd angles, her skin pale as chalk, her shabby blue robe that would have disappeared instantly into the throw-out pile should she ever try to give it to charity.

Perfect. This was so exactly how she wanted to start her day.

Trying—and failing—to find humor in the situation, she walked to the back door and cautiously peeked outside. Sure enough Detective Mark Kincaid stood there, his handsome self dressed in sweats that should have looked horrible but instead made her mouth water. She opened the door.

"Did you have an appointment?" she asked before she could stop herself.

He smiled. Instantly her heart jumped into her

throat and her ability to form whole sentences dove for her toes. It was not a pleasant sensation.

"I've been watching your house, waiting for you to wake up," he said, sliding past her and entering the kitchen. "I figured you'd have to get up early."

She closed the door and pulled her robe more tightly around herself. "Okay. I'm up and you're here. Why?"

Instead of answering, he pulled her against him. She had absolutely no warning and no way to stop his mouth from settling against hers. She told herself to protest, or at the very least, not to melt. Her body didn't listen. Instead of pushing him away, her arms wrapped around him and held on as tightly as his. Instead of yelling out a complaint, her mouth simply softened, then parted to admit him. She went from numb to alive in .8 seconds. He was better than a double latte.

He tasted of mint and coffee, a surprisingly pleasant combination. The fingers of one hand tangled in her messy hair while his other hand rested on her rear. She felt herself both heating and readying, as if they were going to make love this morning. Right here in her kitchen. Was that more or less tacky than the sofa?

"Wait one darn minute!"

She managed to gather a few threads of common sense and shove him away. She kept her gaze fixed firmly on his face, knowing that if she looked down she would see visual proof of what she'd just felt against her stomach.

He swore softly. "Darcy, I'm sorry. That's not why

I'm here." He half turned from her. "I really wanted to talk about last night."

"There's nothing to say."

"Sure there is."

He looked at her and she noticed that while he'd shaved, he hadn't showered. He looked rumpled and too sexy for words. At that moment, she would have sold her soul to be with him. Fortunately, no one appeared with a contract and she was able to at least *act* disinterested.

He stared into her eyes. "About two this morning I realized I'd been completely irresponsible."

Oh. That. "I know." She folded her arms over her chest. "We're both old enough to know better. I can't believe I had unprotected sex."

"I'm sorry. It was my fault."

She wished that were true. If only she could blame all of this on him. "No. I was a party to what went on. I didn't think about it, either."

He took a step toward her. "I'm okay. You won't catch anything from me. But there's another consideration."

For a second she thought he was politely asking about her health status. "I haven't been with anyone in—" She paused before she actually said "years" then continued. "There's no medical condition."

"What about you getting pregnant?"

"It's unlikely. Our timing was fairly safe."

His green eyes seemed to see through her. "Fairly safe isn't a sure thing. You'll let me know if..."

"You'll be the second to know."

"Are you sorry?"

He towered over her—a strong, powerful man. She supposed she should have been afraid, but after last night she knew he was tender and caring. He'd made love to her as if her pleasure had mattered more than his own. It had been an enlightening experience. Now, this morning, she found herself wanting to do it all again, only more slowly.

"No," she said quietly. "I'm a little shocked by our behavior, but I don't regret it."

"I agree."

She wanted to know more. She wanted him to tell her that he found her sexy and irresistible, that he *liked* her as much as he wanted her. She also wanted to win a couple million dollars in the next two weeks.

"Where do we go from here?" he asked.

The question surprised her. For a single heartbeat, she thought about blurting out the truth. That she was lonely and desperately wanted someone in her life. Someone who would care about her and maybe even grow to love her. Someone who wouldn't mind about Dirk. Someone...but not Mark. Her luck wasn't that good.

"I have to take a shower," she said. "I'm due at work in less than an hour. Maybe we could table this discussion until later?"

"Okay." He made no move to leave. "I could help."

"With what?"

He moved closer, then cupped her face and slowly kissed her. The tender touch of his mouth on hers made her legs buckle. She had to grab on to him to stay standing. Heat from his body seemed to surround her own, drawing her in, weaving a spell she couldn't resist.

"With your shower," he murmured. "You know, scrub your back."

"It's just about sex," she said, talking more to herself than him.

"Is that bad?" He reached into his sweats pocket and pulled out a small packet. "I remembered protection this time."

She tried to be outraged that he had arrived at her house with the intention of having sex with her. But before she could muster the words, he was backing her toward her bedroom. Somehow her robe had opened and he was touching her breasts. The feel of his hands on her curves dissolved her fragile indignation, not to mention short-circuiting her self-control. Darn the man. She would give him a piece of her mind, just as soon as they finished making love.

Light spilled from the bathroom, allowing her to see him as he paused in the doorway of her bedroom. He tugged off her robe. She tossed it away. He pulled off his sweatshirt, then kicked off his athletic shoes before stepping out of his sweats. He was naked underneath.

She saw the muscles rippling in his broad chest, the scar on his left side. As much as she wanted to explore the angry, red marks, she was more interested in his jutting arousal. When she started kissing him, she slipped her hand down his side, then around in front until she could touch him.

He pulsed against her questing fingers. So hard and

ready. She felt a clenching deep inside herself at the thought of him filling her.

"Shower," he said against her mouth, kissing her and guiding her backward at the same time.

He drew her nightgown over her head and tossed it to the ground. Her panties quickly followed. She heard the rush of water but barely paid attention because now he was slipping his fingers between her legs and touching her in that special way of his. By the time they stepped under the steamy stray, she was nearly ready to climax.

He lathered her all over, paying particular attention to her breasts. He teased her nipples until she was panting. She responded by grabbing the soap and rubbing *him* all over. When she slipped her hands between his legs, he groaned. They washed each other's hair, letting the soapy water pour off them as they kissed.

Mark reached for the condom he'd left on the vanity, then slipped it on. Darcy glanced doubtfully around at the tub.

"How exactly did you plan on us..."

He smiled. "Trust me."

He turned her so that her back was to him. She didn't mind because he nibbled down her neck and reached around to play with her breasts. When she was trembling and desperate, he urged to her raise one leg so her foot rested on the rim of the tub. Something hard probed at her from behind.

Instinctively she bent forward. As he entered her, filling her and making her gasp, he slipped one hand around and began to rub against her most sensitive place. His fingers matched the pace of his thrusting, robbing her of will. She braced her hands against the wall of the tub. The cold tile contrasted with the heat they generated between them.

Faster and faster, everything so incredibly perfect until she had no choice but to surrender to the climax. As her body began to shudder, she felt him stiffen. He breathed her name as they both spent themselves in the glory of their joining.

"At least the cleanup was easy," Darcy muttered to herself as she drove to the Hip Hop Café twenty minutes later.

She avoided glancing at the clock in the dash—she already knew that she was late. She couldn't believe it. After five years of near-perfect behavior, she'd lost control twice in less than twenty-four hours—and with the same man. Although she supposed that was better than losing control with a different man. Apparently all she had to do was avoid Mark and she could return to her previously calm, if lonely, existence.

She couldn't believe they'd done it again. She also couldn't believe how good it had been. In her past, lovemaking had been something the man wanted. She had enjoyed herself on rare occasions but she'd never felt the earth move. Nor had she ever done it in the shower, or in that particular position. It had been—she shivered—delightful.

She pulled into the back parking lot of the Hip Hop. There were three other employee cars there, along with four belonging to customers. She breathed a sigh of relief. At least it was the morning after Thanksgiving and most people were going to still be too stuffed with turkey to bother with breakfast out. Trying not to notice it was six thirty-five, she grabbed her purse and dove out of the car.

"I know, I know," she said as she entered the alcove with the lockers and quickly put away her things. She looked at Janie and sighed. "I'm twenty minutes late. I'm really sorry."

Janie shrugged off her apology. "Darcy, this is the first time in what—six months? We're not even busy. I think I can cut you some slack."

"Thanks. It won't happen again."

At least she didn't think it would. She couldn't imagine Mark showing up at her door to make love with her every morning. Although the thought of that made her heat up in the best way possible.

"How was your Thanksgiving?" her boss asked.

Darcy tied on her apron and tried not to blush. "Great," she said, hurrying toward the front of the café. Janie followed. "I'd planned on having several people over. Mostly ones with nowhere to go on the holiday. But everyone canceled on me so Mark Kincaid was my only guest."

She grabbed a pot of coffee and quickly made a swing through the restaurant. There were only three occupied tables, along with a single man at the counter. Everyone already had food, except for one couple ready to order. She wrote their requests onto her pad, then delivered the information to the kitchen.

Janie was waiting for her back by the coffeemaker. Her long blond ponytail swished like a horse's tail as she shook her head. "Excuse me, but did you say Mark Kincaid?"

Darcy smiled and prayed that she didn't look guilty. "Uh-huh. He lives next door to me and he's a regular here. I don't see him with a lot of people so I thought he might be alone for the holiday. This time of year can be tough on people who don't have family locally."

Janie stared at her as if she were crazy. "So you just invited him over?"

"Uh-huh."

"And he just accepted?"

Darcy tried to act casual. "Sure. Why wouldn't he?"

"I don't know. Since he moved back to Whitehorn, Mark hasn't exactly been social." Janie's expression turned speculative. "Anything interesting to report?"

"Gee, he's really nice."

"And?"

Darcy held her gaze and shrugged. "And what? Like I said, he's a nice guy. Kind of quiet. Hates vegetables."

Janie laughed. "I'm not surprised. He always refuses a salad when he comes in for lunch or dinner. I didn't know you knew him." Her humor faded. "I'm glad he joined you for Thanksgiving. If you hadn't invited him over, I suspect he would have been alone."

Darcy glanced around to make sure her customers didn't need her, then lowered her voice. "I know he doesn't have family in town. I get the impression he doesn't have much family anywhere."

"Just his sister, Maddie. His parents died when he was in college." Janie paused, as if trying to remember. "There was another relative. A great-aunt, I think. Mark took care of Maddie until he graduated from college, then his aunt took over so he could go to New York."

Darcy tried not to read too much into the information. So Mark had taken care of his sister. They had that in common, but little else. "Where is Maddie now?"

"On the road somewhere. She's a barrel racer and travels around to the different rodeos. She doesn't get back here much."

The door to the café opened and two couples entered. Darcy seated them, then took their orders. By then she had food to deliver, coffee to refill and more customers to serve. It might not be as busy as a regular workday, but she was the only waitress on duty.

She was nearly an hour into her shift when she felt the hairs on the back of her neck stand up. She was in the process of buttering toast and the bread nearly slipped from her fingers. Even knowing what she was going to see, she couldn't help turning around.

Sure enough, Mark Kincaid had just walked into the Hip Hop Café. Across the worn linoleum and a half dozen or so people, they stared at each other. There was something in his eyes—a connection built by remembered passion—that made her insides go up in flames.

Don't go there, she warned herself. Men like him were heartbreak city. But while her head was very willing to listen to the excellent advice, the rest of her body wasn't willing to be so cooperative.

Chapter Five

Mark slid into his usual booth. Except for the slight twinkle in his eye and the faint smile teasing the corners of his mouth, he looked completely normal. Darcy was envious. If only she felt that way. Her stomach had taken up permanent residence in her toes and her hands actually shook as she grabbed the coffeepot and made her way to his table.

"Good morning," she mumbled, not able to meet his gaze. She poured coffee, careful not to spill. "Have you decided, or do you need a few minutes?"

"Good morning, Darcy."

She finished pouring and forced herself to look at him. His smile broadened.

"How are you this morning?" he asked.

Under other circumstances it could be considered a reasonable question, but this situation was anything but normal. After all, less than two hours before, they'd been making passionate love in her shower. Last night…

She swallowed, not wanting to think about last night and all the things they'd done.

"I'm, um, what was the question?"

His smile took on a very self-satisfied quality that made her want to smack him. He looked like what he was—a smug male who had just recently sexually pleased a woman.

"About your order?" She grabbed her pad and pencil from her apron.

"The usual. Western omelette, side of bacon. You've already brought me the coffee."

Her protest was automatic. "Mark, you can't keep eating like this. It's so unhealthy. Aren't you worried about dying young or getting heart disease?"

He leaned close. Instinctively she did the same, shifting so that their faces were only a few inches apart.

"I appreciate the concern," he murmured. "However, in the past day or so, I've had a lot of extra exercise and I really need to keep up my strength."

She glared at him, unable to believe what he'd just said. At the same time, heat flared in her cheeks and she knew that she was blushing. The man could be really annoying…in the most charming way possible.

She turned to leave. He stopped her with a light touch on her arm.

"Why don't you bring me some pumpkin bread, too. I enjoyed it the last time I had some. Even if it *is* made with vegetables."

She hated that he complimented her cooking, mostly because it made her go all soft and mushy inside.

"You're not playing fair," she protested.

"I know."

She walked off without saying anything else. There were more customers who needed her attention and she really had to get away from Mark before she said or did something stupid.

It had been a lot of years since she'd had to deal with the awkwardness of "the morning after." She remembered the time as being fraught with peril. Apparently her time out of the dating game hadn't changed that particular fact.

Darcy took orders from new customers, delivered hot food and avoided Mark right up until his breakfast was ready. Then she had no choice but to return to his table. She set down the plate with the omelette, along with two smaller dishes containing the bacon and pumpkin bread.

"Thanks," he said. "Everything looks great."

"I'll pass along the compliment."

"Especially you."

Her heart did a quick double beat. "Mark, don't."

"Why not? It's true." He leaned toward her. "How about tonight?"

Her insides quivered. Did she want this? Him in her house…in her? Heat poured through her at the thought. Impulses weren't a part of her current life, so why was she so quick to give in now? She wanted to tell herself that she was crazy. She felt crazy. But she also felt excited about something other than finding Dirk a good school for the first time in years. Was that so bad?

"Darcy?"

"I'm thinking."

"I didn't imagine the question would be so hard."

"Well, it is."

"Why?"

Because he represented temptation, she thought. The question was how would she pay for giving in? Darcy knew any relationship with Mark, even one primarily located in the bedroom, was going to cost her a lot.

Did she mind that? The problem was she'd been so lonely for so long. Mark made her remember that she was still alive and very much a woman. Shouldn't she be allowed to have a temporary diversion in her life?

A sound at the door interrupted her musings. She looked up and saw Homer Gilmore wander into the café. He glanced around fearfully, as if expecting someone to pounce. Darcy turned to Janie, who looked as concerned and undecided as she, Darcy, felt.

Homer was the town eccentric. Well into his seventies and losing his faculties, he often wandered around town, talking to himself. He was usually harmless, but with his long gray hair, slippers and bathrobe, he was just enough outside of normal to be scary.

Darcy squared her shoulders and approached the old man. "Morning, Mr. Gilmore," she said cheerfully. "Can I get you something?"

Homer glared at her, muttering something she

couldn't understand. Out of the corner of her eye, she saw Janie heading for the phone, no doubt to call Homer's nurse to come and get him.

"I'll take care of this."

The familiar voice caught her by surprise. Darcy turned as Mark approached. He gently took Homer by the arm.

"Come on, Mr. Gilmore. I'm with the sheriff's office. Mark Kincaid. Why don't I see you home?"

Homer glared at him, then his wild eyes cleared slightly and he nodded.

"Can you wrap up my breakfast?" Mark asked. "I'll pick it up on my way back. I'll pay my bill then, too."

"No problem. It's not as if I don't know where you live."

He grabbed his jacket and shrugged into it, then ushered Homer out of the Hip Hop. Darcy watched them go. Her chest tightened, but with more than nervousness and anticipation. She could accept Mark being handsome, sexy and very good in bed. What she didn't want was for him to be nice. If she thought he was a decent guy, and charming, she would have a whole lot more trouble keeping her emotions in check and her heart on a very short leash.

She reminded herself that the last thing she needed was to fall for a guy. She knew what happened when she did. There was no point in wishing this time would be different.

Mark kept his finger on the channel button of the remote. He was clicking through stations so quickly there was no way he could see what was on. But flipping through the offerings was better than pacing. Which is what he really wanted to do.

He glanced at his watch, then back at the television. Five-forty. When he'd returned to the Hip Hop to pick up his breakfast, Darcy had agreed to see him that night. He'd told her he would be over at six. As they lived in the same building, there was no way he could justify leaving early to beat traffic.

To think that the previous day he'd been dreading going there for Thanksgiving. He'd thought he would be bored and out of place. He thought she wasn't anything but a do-gooder with a plan to rule the world with tofu. He'd been wrong.

She'd been smart and funny, not to mention incredibly sexy. He hadn't planned on making love with her, but he couldn't be sorry that it had happened. Not yesterday or this morning.

His body stirred at the memory of their time in her shower. She had the ability to turn him on in a nanosecond. He'd never experienced anything like it before.

He leaned back in his chair, releasing the remote so the television stayed on a sports channel. This brief sex-only relationship with Darcy was exactly what he needed. With Sylvia he'd thought he'd found "the one." He'd wanted to settle down, marry her and have a couple of kids. She'd shown him that dreams like that were for idiots.

Without meaning to, he remembered Sylvia smiling at him the first time they'd met. He'd thought she'd

been as taken with him as he'd been with her. With
the distance and wisdom of hindsight, he realized that
every movement, every touch, every word had been
calculated. She'd had a goal when she'd "accidentally" locked herself out of her place and had used
his phone to call the locksmith. He'd been the sucker
to fall in with her plans.

He'd learned the lesson well. Love wasn't a part
of his plan. But sex. That was something else entirely.
For the first time since the shooting he felt himself
anticipating something other than the absence of pain.

He was returning to life. That it was happening
wasn't much of a surprise. It had been inevitable. The
how was something else. Darcy was an unexpected
pleasure. He would enjoy this while it lasted and then
move on. Never again would he allow his heart to be
engaged.

Darcy frantically hung discarded outfits back on
hangers. She'd changed her clothes five times in the
past thirty minutes and she was determined not to do
it again. What did it matter what she had on? Mark
wasn't coming over to see her dressed…he was far
more interested in having her undressed. This was all
about sex. She had on her best bra-and-panty set to
prove it. She was having an adult relationship based
purely on physical attraction. People did it all the
time. It was very sophisticated.

It was also very not her.

Darcy sank onto the bed and covered her face with
her hands. What was she doing? While she felt excited and quivery at the thought of Mark coming over

in a few minutes, she also felt empty inside. Empty and cheap and bad about herself. The feeling was oddly familiar and it took her several seconds to figure out when she'd last experienced the sensation.

Before her parents had died, she thought sadly. Back when she'd been shallow and selfish, living only for the moment. Back when the kind of car a guy drove was far more important than something like honesty or compassion. When looks had mattered more than character. She dropped her hands to her sides.

She'd worked hard to change herself. While the initial plunge into the world of reality had come at the hand of circumstance, once she'd been forced to face her own lacking character, she had done her best to do better. Five years later, she could honestly say she was proud of who she was.

Was she proud after last night or this morning?

The lovemaking had been incredible. Darcy had forgotten what it was like to have a man touch her bare skin—to feel his body next to hers, entering hers. She'd been starved and Mark had fed her. But now what? Did she really want to have an affair with a man she barely knew? Or did she want something more?

She wasn't crazy enough to think she was searching for true love. She had her doubts about being lucky enough to find someone who would adore her *and* be willing to deal with Dirk. She knew her brother was an amazing person, but not everyone could look past his developmental issues to see the gentle heart inside.

So she'd given up on the fairy tale, instead resigning herself to a life alone. The move to Whitehorn had cut her off from her hard-won support group. She needed to make friends, finding people she could both like and trust.

But would Mark be interested in being a friend or was he only in it for what he could get?

Mark knocked on Darcy's front door at exactly two minutes before six. He'd wanted to wait until a couple of minutes past, but he'd been too eager, too aroused. He'd already imagined her opening the door and ushering him inside. He'd thought of gathering her in his arms and kissing her until they were both breathless with passion.

But reality didn't live up to fantasy. For one thing, Darcy wasn't smiling when she opened her door. For another, she wouldn't look at him.

Her whispered hello did little to alleviate the sudden ache in his gut.

"What's wrong?" he asked as she stepped into her living room.

"Nothing." She brushed her hands against her black slacks and motioned for him to take à seat on the sofa.

He hesitated. While he appreciated the polite gesture, he couldn't help remembering that twenty-four hours before they'd been making love on that same piece of furniture.

"Darcy?"

She crossed to the window and parted the blinds to look out. "I'm fine, Mark. It's just..." Her voice trailed off. She glanced at him, then away. "You're not going to like this."

The bad feeling got worse. "Why don't you say it and let me be the judge?"

She nodded, still without looking at him. Her short, blond hair was a mass of curls. Lamplight brought out the shades of gold in the strands. One small hand lingered on the blinds.

"I can't do the sex thing," she said without warning. "I know it doesn't make sense to you. We've done it twice, so what's the big deal, right? I mean it's a new century and we're all contemporary single people. Except I'm not. I didn't mean to have old-fashioned values. I didn't even know that I had them. Suddenly they were just there." She glanced at him over her shoulder. "I'm sorry. You probably want to go now."

Mark tried not to think about the two condoms in his back pocket. He shoved his hands into his front pockets and stared at her back.

"What changed your mind?" he asked.

She shrugged. "I didn't like what I was thinking about myself. I'm not saying I didn't enjoy the sex…I did, it was great. But there has to be more."

He turned away and swore under his breath. This was just his luck, he thought grimly. He wanted sex and she wanted… He didn't know but he was sure he wouldn't like it. She was right—he should leave. Except, somehow, leaving seemed like the wrong thing to do.

"Mark?"

"What?"

"You can go. Really. It's okay. You didn't ask me out or anything. We have no emotional connection or hint of commitment between us. My inviting you here for Thanksgiving was entirely my idea. You don't owe me anything."

"I know."

He did know. Yet he couldn't seem to get his feet heading for the door.

He reminded himself he wasn't looking for a relationship. He couldn't ever trust her; he wasn't interested in falling in love.

"What do you want?" he asked before he could stop himself.

She turned slowly, until she was facing him. Something that might have been hope flared to life in her eyes.

"I thought maybe we could be friends."

Her voice was small as she spoke, as if she knew she was asking for the moon and she didn't doubt he was going to laugh at her.

He reminded himself he wasn't looking for entanglements and that she was a woman with secrets. Not that he'd cared at five-twenty that morning.

"Friends?" he repeated.

She nodded. "Nothing romantic," she added hastily, making him perversely want to know why not. "Just friends."

He didn't say anything. Darcy swallowed. "I know that sounds weird, but I've been really busy since I moved here and I don't really know that many people. You and I seem to get along, even outside the bedroom."

She sounded sincere. He even almost believed her. Friends. It wasn't anything he'd considered. There were complications. He didn't want to get involved, and ironically a sex-only relationship had seemed far less trouble. Friends implied more than he was willing to give.

He knew he should tell her he wasn't interested, but for some reason he couldn't speak the words. Maybe it was because he'd been on his own since he'd returned to Whitehorn. He'd been meaning to look up old buddies, but somehow he never found the time. Besides, what was he supposed to say to them?

"Why not romance?" he asked. "Not with me, but with someone?"

She gave a rueful smile. "I don't have really good luck with men."

Her statement made him want to ask a half-dozen questions, but he didn't. If they were just going to be friends, why did her past matter?

"We can give it a try," he said at last.

"Really?" She smiled, her full mouth curving up, her eyes brightening with pleasure. "Great."

"I do have a question."

"What?"

"How do you plan to avoid temptation?"

Her smile faded slightly. "Yes, well, that is a concern, isn't it? I suppose I won't think about it."

"What if I start to seduce you?"

Her steady gaze met his. "I don't think I'd be able to stop you. I guess I'm going to have to risk it. Do you plan to seduce me?"

He shook his head and it was only half a lie.

Strangely, it was enough for her to admit that he could easily tempt her into his bed.

"I'm depending on you to be a gentleman," she murmured.

He groaned. "That hardly seems fair."

"Imagine how I feel. I've just admitted you have all that power."

They faced each other—still standing in the living room. Mark didn't know about her, but he felt damned awkward.

"Now what?" he asked.

"It's up to you. I have all the fixings for a great turkey stir-fry. We could have dinner and talk about our first friendship project."

"We're going to have projects?"

"Sure. Don't guys like to get together to do things, while women like to sit around and talk? I thought we could start with something that would make you feel more comfortable."

"Like what?"

"There's a decorating party at the children's wing of the hospital. I thought we'd go there."

Damn do-gooder, he grumbled to himself. Typical.

"No way, no how," he announced.

Darcy only smiled.

Chapter Six

Mark still couldn't believe he was here, in the hospital, about to decorate a tree. It was humiliating.

"Don't you know I'm a tough cop?" he muttered in Darcy's ear. "I'm supposed to be out subduing criminals, not participating in a decorating seminar."

Darcy didn't look the least bit impressed by his protests. "You agreed to this last night. It's fun, it's for a good cause, so quit complaining."

They were in the main waiting area of the children's wing. Several other people gathered around, listening to the director's instructions. Mark recognized Janie from the Hip Hop Café, along with one of the younger deputies.

"You'll break into groups of two or three," the woman was saying. "The trees are on various floors. We've distributed the decorations as well, and the children who are mobile have been told they're welcome to help.''

Mark felt trapped by circumstances. He hadn't been thinking when he'd agreed to this. He wasn't the tree-decorating type. He'd been avoiding polite society since he'd arrived back in Whitehorn and now he felt out of place.

By contrast, Darcy practically quivered with anticipation. ''Isn't this great?'' she asked as they made their way to the elevator to take them to the fourth floor. Their tree was close to the playroom.

As they stepped onto the floor, familiar smells assaulted Mark. He'd spent too long in a hospital, not to mention rehab, after he'd been shot. He remembered bad meals, no sleep and plenty of pain. They weren't good memories. As they passed open doors leading to patients' rooms, he saw small children hooked up to IVs and lying still in bed when they should have been home running and jumping and laughing.

All those years as a New York City detective and a bunch of sick kids still got to him. Damn. He'd gone soft.

''Okay, so let's see what ornaments we have,'' Darcy said when they reached the bare Christmas tree in the corner by the entrance to the playroom. It was tall and the scent of pine helped overcome the smell of illness.

''We'll sort them by type and color, then come up with a plan.''

He stared at her as she crouched next to the boxes of ornaments. ''We need a plan?''

"Absolutely. We can't just hang things wherever we want."

"Why not?"

She didn't even bother answering. Instead she rolled her eyes, as if he were being too dumb for words.

"I never realized you were such a control freak," he said.

"I'm not. Well, sometimes. If I can't always control the big things in my life, I tend to micromanage the little things. Decorating for Christmas is one of them. Maybe it's because I've been responsible for doing it on my own since my folks died."

Darcy emptied the contents of all the boxes. When Mark squatted next to her, she handed him containers of wooden ornaments with instructions for him to sort them by size. She examined their strings of lights, even going so far as to lay them out in the empty playroom to calculate the exact length of each.

"You go to all this trouble at home?" he asked when she'd returned with the announcement that there were probably enough lights, but they were going to have to be careful to make sure every branch had a decoration.

"Absolutely. Decorating my tree is an entire weekend affair."

He started to tease her that he would like to be out of town during that time, but the words got stuck in his throat. He had a feeling that he would enjoy spending that weekend with Darcy. She might even be able to exorcise some of his demons.

"Whatcha doin'?"

The soft voice came from behind him. Mark turned to see a small girl standing by the edge of the hall. She wore a worn pink bathrobe and cat slippers. One hand clutched a tattered teddy while the other held on to a kid-size IV stand. Two plastic bags dripped into lines that disappeared up her sleeve.

"We're decorating the tree," Darcy said with a smile. "I was thinking about putting her on top. What do you think?"

As Darcy spoke, she held up a white-and-gold angel. The little girl had a scarf over her head. Her eyebrows were gone, as were her eyelashes. But judging from the freckles marching across her pert nose, Mark guessed that she was a redhead.

The child tilted her head as she studied the angel. "She's pretty," she said.

"I agree." Darcy nodded. "Okay. We'll put her on top and tomorrow you can tell everyone it was your idea."

The girl smiled shyly.

"What's your name?" Darcy asked.

"Brittany."

"Do you want to help?"

Brittany hesitated, then shook her head. "I'm gonna get a second chemo and it makes me throw up. But I'll come see the tree tomorrow."

Darcy nodded without speaking. Mark saw tears in her eyes.

Brittany waved, then turned and headed back toward her room.

Mark watched her go. "Now I see why you do this."

Darcy sniffed, then cleared her throat. "I want to help. I don't have a lot of money, so I can't give very much."

"Time can be more precious."

She returned to sorting the ornaments. "No one should be in the hospital at Christmas. If they have to be, we owe it to them to make it special. The holidays are a time for connecting."

He wondered who she would be spending the holidays with. After all, her parents were gone and she hadn't had any family at Thanksgiving diner.

But he didn't ask. There were things about her he didn't want to know. They implied a closeness that made him uncomfortable. He was still adjusting to the fact that he'd agreed to be her friend. Growing up in Whitehorn, he'd never been much of a joiner. Since returning the only thing he'd gotten involved with was a weekly Sunday morning basketball game.

"What has you looking so serious?" Darcy asked.

"I was just thinking that I never fit in around here. I didn't get the whole cowboy thing."

"That's really interesting. I mean, considering your sister tours with the rodeo."

He stared at her. "How did you know about my sister?"

"I, ah, well..." Darcy stood and studied the tree. "We should really do the lights now."

"Not so fast." He grabbed her arm and turned her to face him. "Who told you about Maddie?"

"It wasn't anything." She stared at the center of his chest. "There was some talk about you when you returned to town and I might have recently mentioned you to Janie. I *had* issued a rather impulsive invitation to my house for Thanksgiving and I wanted to make sure you weren't dangerous. At least not in the criminal sense.''

He leaned close. ''You didn't realize I'd be so irresistible in bed.''

She raised her gaze to his. ''You have an overinflated ego.''

''You were the one screaming my name.''

She blinked first. ''The lights.''

''Lead the way.''

They started at the top of the tree. Mark positioned the strands while Darcy gave instructions. He enjoyed the sound of her voice and the fact that she'd been curious enough to ask around about him.

When the lights were arranged to her picky satisfaction, they switched to ornaments. Despite her diminutive stature, Darcy insisted on hanging decorations near the top of the tree. She had to stand on tiptoe to reach, which meant her sweater crept up, exposing a strip of bare back and belly. Mark stood back and enjoyed the view. As he wasn't likely to get any from her anytime soon, he would take what crumbs he could find.

They argued over where to place painted gingerbread men, and he deliberately moved several paper cranes to a different branch. Outraged, Darcy planted her hands on her hips.

''I cannot work under these conditions,'' she exclaimed, raising her voice slightly when she caught sight of a boy on crutches. He was about nine or ten, and thin.

Dramatically Darcy tossed her head, then stared at the heavens. "I am an artist. You must not disrupt my flow."

"I'm going to get out of the way before I step in it," Mark muttered under his breath.

The boy laughed.

Mark inched toward him, then dropped into a crouch. "Women," he said. "Do they drive you crazy, too?"

The boy nodded.

Mark pulled two more wooden ornaments out of his shirt pocket. "I'll distract her and you hang these, okay?"

Big brown eyes brightened at the thought of a conspiracy. Mark sensed Darcy's attention and knew that she'd heard him, but that wasn't a problem. He didn't doubt she would play along with the game.

"Oh, Darcy," he said, his voice loud enough to carry. "We're missing a box of ornaments."

She turned toward him, careful to keep her back to the boy who was moving slowly toward the tree.

"Did you lose them again? I thought I could trust you. Where did you last see the box?"

Mark rose and shrugged. "I don't know. Maybe *you* lost them."

"Me?" She pressed a hand to her chest. "I'm crushed you would say such a thing about me. Simply crushed. Mortified. Broken."

She sagged into a nearby chair and buried her head in her hands. The child finished hanging the two ornaments and made his way to Mark's side.

"Good job," Mark said, touching the boy's shoulder. "I'm impressed."

Darcy looked at the tree and sprang to her feet. "My tree. It's perfect. And yet. No! Someone has touched it. Someone has...made it better. Was it you?"

She turned to the boy. He grinned in delight. She returned to her chair.

"Done in by a child."

Still smiling, the boy gave a little wave then started back to his room. One of the nurses stepped into the hall.

"Jon-Anthony, you get back here, young man. You just got your crutches today and already you're running marathons. I told the doctor you'd be trouble, but did she listen?"

"Nice job," Darcy said, rising and surveying their tree. "You're really good with kids."

"You, too."

They stared at each other. It was too much like a moment for Mark to be comfortable. "Maddie was always breaking something when we were growing up. It was never fun for her to be slowed down by a cast or crutches. I used to entertain her."

Darcy stared down the hall. "I feel badly for the children who have to spend Christmas here."

"You're helping."

"I want it to be enough, and I'm not sure it is."

She looked a little lost as she spoke. He had the thought she was the kind of woman who should be married with a couple of kids of her own. That might keep her from wanting to rescue the world.

As he stared at the lights on the tree, he remembered when he'd had his own dreams about children. It had been a year ago, right after he'd met Sylvia. By their second date, he'd been ready to propose, having already named their children. He'd never been happier.

Suddenly he could hear the sound of Sylvia's laughter. He recalled how she'd looked waiting for him to come home from work. Usually she'd been naked and in his bed. It had taken nearly three months after he'd gotten out of the hospital for him to stop expecting to see her. Even when he'd stopped caring about her, she'd still managed to invade his dreams. Even now she haunted him, reminding him to be wary.

"Mark?"

He turned to look at Darcy.

"Want to come back to earth?" she asked with a smile.

"Sorry."

Suddenly he was uncomfortable in his own skin. He recognized the feeling, hating it, knowing that there wasn't anything he could do about it except wait it out. His bullet wounds began to ache and he wished it wasn't so cold out. He needed to go for a run.

"I should go," he said, grateful he'd met her at the hospital so he could make a quick exit. Who knew the ghosts would follow him back to Whitehorn?

"Are you all right?" she asked. "You look—I don't know—unhappy."

"I'm fine. I just need to get home."

She nodded. "Do you still want me to come to your basketball game tomorrow?"

He'd nearly forgotten. "Sure. Eight-thirty sharp."

She groaned. "Sunday is my only day to sleep in."

He pointed at the tree and she sighed.

"I'll be there," she promised.

As he walked to his truck, he found himself oddly pleased by the fact that she was coming to watch the game. All he had to do now was survive the night and not let the demons win.

Darcy arrived at the basketball courts a little before eight-thirty. She came bearing gifts. Something about the way Mark had left the hospital the previous night had made her uncomfortable. She wanted to make things right between them—difficult to do when she wasn't sure anything was wrong. Regardless, she used the only fix that she knew was bound to work with a bunch of guys playing sports.

Cinnamon rolls.

The smell of the freshly baked breakfast treat nearly made her crazy while she drove the few miles between her place and the new gym facility. But she'd been determined to resist. Eating with the guys would be her bonding experience.

She parked next to Mark's truck, trying not to think that they could have easily gone together. But he hadn't offered and she hadn't wanted to ask. He'd accepted her request that they be friends instead of lovers, although she'd sensed that wasn't his first choice. She didn't want to push things. Telling herself she'd done fine all this time without Mark in her life was interesting but not convincing. Darn the man for starting to get under her skin.

She carried her pink box of goodies, along with a couple of carafes of coffee and several disposable cups, into the main entrance, then headed for the gym. She followed the sound of male voices and laughter into one of the practice areas. Once inside the warm room, she came to a stop—overwhelmed by so much masculinity in a single room.

She recognized Mark right away. In fact her gaze sought him out first, as if he contained a homing beacon she'd been especially programmed to find. She barely noticed the other guys milling around. They all looked good enough in their loose gym shorts and baggy T-shirts, but only Mark made her heart beat the tiniest bit faster.

He looked up and saw her. In that split second, she held her breath, hoping for a flash of desire to harden his expression. Unfortunately, he kept whatever he was feeling to himself, although he did grin at her and wave her over.

"Hey, Darcy, what's in the box?"

She glared at him. "What's in the box? Not 'Hi' or 'Nice to see you'?"

Josh Anderson, the owner of Anderson, Inc., strolled over. "Morning, Darcy. Nice to see you. What's in the box?"

She turned her back on Mark. "Some people have manners. Some people take the time to be appreciative. Good morning, Josh. I made cinnamon rolls and brought coffee."

"The woman's a goddess," he said, reaching to

take the box from her and opening the top. Instantly the sweet scent surrounded them.

Mark moved close. "Josh only *thinks* you're a goddess. I happen to know that it's true."

"Oh, please." Darcy wrinkled her nose to show she wasn't the least bit impressed, this despite the quivering in her stomach and thighs.

The guys ate nearly all the cinnamon rolls and gulped most of the coffee. Then Mark grabbed a basketball from the rack and the game began.

Darcy settled herself on the side bleachers to watch. The men were aggressive, pushing and shoving, cheering their scores and booing their opponents. When the ball bounced in her direction, she tossed it back, earning a quick wink from one of the players. A couple of loud swearwords earned a "ladies present" comment from Josh. Even Mark teased her about doing a cheer or two for his team.

Darcy sipped her coffee and enjoyed the feeling of belonging. She knew it was temporary, but for the moment, it was very nice. She hadn't had all that much belonging in the past five years. She'd been so busy working to keep herself and Dirk afloat that she hadn't had time for a regular life. All the strays in the world weren't going to make up for that.

Listening to the male laughter made her think of her brother. She hoped he was having a good time in Chicago. She would go see him next week and hear all about his trip.

According to Andrew, the counselor at the school, Dirk was doing a good job of making friends. He'd found his place in the world, at least for the next few years. Darcy could finally draw a breath and relax about Dirk. All she had to worry about now was making sure there was enough money to pay for the school, and that was the easy part. Over the past few years she'd learned that she had a capacity for hard work.

She'd also learned that she was a pretty caring person. She liked giving to others, whether it was helping at the hospital or having people with nowhere else to go over to her house for a holiday meal. She liked—

Darcy blinked as Mark made a basket. In the middle of her self-congratulation party she had the sudden thought that, while she was very willing to open her life to people in need, she rarely opened her heart. Except for Dirk, everyone else she'd known or had made friends with had been someone moving on. Just by calling people "her strays," she invited distance in the relationship. She didn't have any close friends here in Whitehorn. She wanted to blame that on her time in town—it had only been six months. But it wasn't that. Who had she been close to in Arizona?

So why had she stayed so solitary, she wondered. What had made her pull back? The humiliation of what had happened after her parents died? The need to stay in control? Was she punishing herself for being so self-absorbed while she was growing up?

She didn't have any answers, which was depressing. After all, she was twenty-five. Shouldn't she have her life together by now?

No answer came to her so she focused her attention on the game. It finished with a mad attack by Mark's team. Three baskets in succession gave them the victory.

He grabbed a towel from his gym bag and collapsed next to her on the bench. "Pretty impressive, huh?" he said, draping the towel around his neck and wiping his face.

"I was immobilized by awe," she teased. "Your physical prowess puts lesser men to shame."

"I know."

She laughed and he grinned at her. The connection between them flared again. The one that made her nervous.

A couple of the guys stopped by to thank her again for the cinnamon rolls. "My pleasure," she told them.

Mark grabbed the last one from the box and took a bite. "What are you doing with the rest of your day?"

"Baking. I have to be prepared for the week. I want to get everything ready for the Hip Hop."

"That's right. You're hoping to be their new supplier." He sipped some cold coffee. "When are you going to find the time to fill their order if you get the contract? Will you quit your waitressing job?"

"No way." She needed the money too much. "If I have to, I'll give up sleep."

He leaned toward her and kissed her on the cheek. "Not bad for some rich girl from the burbs."

"Thanks."

His green-eyed gaze was steady. "I mean it, Darcy. You're impressive."

His compliment made her feel all fluttery inside.

"Well, I do what has to be done." She wondered

what he would say if he knew about Dirk. No doubt he would admire her more and want to be with her less.

"Come on," he said. "I'll walk you to your car."

She started to shrug into her jacket. Mark came up behind her to help. It was a polite gesture that meant little, yet she found herself wanting to believe that it was significant. Like the brief kiss on her cheek. She wanted to think he cared. Which meant she had to watch herself. Obviously she was vulnerable in a very dangerous way—and the last thing she wanted was to fall for a guy who was bound to leave her once he learned the truth about her life.

Mark headed into the office shortly before noon. On Sunday afternoons the place was empty, except for someone stuck on duty answering the phone. He made his way to his messy desk and began sorting through files. One of these days he was going to get his paperwork under control. The problem was he hated it, so he wasn't motivated. Sheriff Rafe Rawlings frequently threatened to set his desk on fire, but Mark wasn't impressed.

Now he leaned back in his chair and surveyed the piles. Maybe he should shove everything into a box and start over with a clean surface. Or maybe—

The phone rang. He pounced on it, delighted with the thought of a reprieve.

"Kincaid."

"Hey, Mark, it's Ralph Wayne. What's going on in Hicksville?"

"Ralph!" Mark rested his elbows on the desk and

grinned. "Still hanging out in vice, hoping to get lucky?"

"You should talk. You're out in Montana. What's the big crime of the day? The cows didn't come home?"

"Yeah, but I caught 'em, and they're doing their time."

Both men laughed.

"How's Sal?" Mark asked, picturing his large friend's petite wife. "Or has she left you yet?"

"You wish. She's great, and so are the kids. Ralph Junior is nearly ten."

"No way."

"It's true. Last week a girl called the house and wanted to talk to him. I nearly had a heart attack."

Ralph was a devoted husband and father. Mark had always admired his friend's ability to keep the job away from his family. When Ralph left the police station every evening, he was a hundred percent with his wife and kids. Mark had spent many happy evenings with the Wayne family.

"So what's new at the department?" Mark asked.

Ralph hesitated. "Actually, that's why I called. I've got some news."

Mark stiffened. "Sylvia?"

"Yeah."

"Did she change her plea again? Wasn't the last one innocent by reason of insanity? Or is it time for me to come back?"

Mark didn't want it to be the latter. He knew that Sylvia would do whatever she could to avoid trial for as long as possible, but eventually she would run out of options. He wasn't looking forward to returning to New York to testify against her or having their private life played out in such a public forum.

When he'd first come back to Whitehorn, he hadn't wanted to see her again because he couldn't believe how wrong he'd been about her. Now he didn't want to see her because she no longer mattered. He'd done his best to put her and her actions behind him. He wanted to move on.

"It's not about the plea," Ralph said. "It's...oh, hell, Mark. I don't know a good way to say this. She's dead. She killed herself."

Chapter Seven

Mark heard the words but didn't believe them.

"Mark?" Ralph asked. "Are you there?"

"Yeah, I'm here."

"I'm sorry."

Mark didn't know what *he* was. Shocked, maybe.
Stunned. His chest hurt, as if he couldn't catch his
breath.

Dead. Sylvia was dead. She'd finally found a way
to avoid being punished for what she'd done. He'd
known she would go to extremes, but this? Was it
possible? Had she simply given up or had this been
part of a plan?

"I don't know what to say," Ralph admitted. "I
didn't want to tell you this over the phone, but—"

"Don't sweat it," Mark told him, finding it diffi-

cult to speak. "I'm glad you were the one who called.
I gotta go. Give my love to Sal."

"You gonna be okay?"

"Sure."

Mark didn't know if he was lying or not as he hung
up the phone. Dead. Sylvia was dead. He tried to
figure out what, if anything, he was feeling.

His body felt entirely empty. As if everything that
had already gone on before had drained him of all
emotion. Unfortunately, the space quickly filled. He
closed his eyes to block out what had happened before, but the action didn't help. Memories swamped
him until he was drowning in the past.

He'd met Sylvia about three months after he'd
moved into a new apartment. She'd been his next-
door neighbor. He still recalled rounding the corner
and finding her balancing too many packages while
she dug in her purse for her keys that hadn't been
there. She'd been a pure New York woman cliché—
tall, thin, dark hair, dressed in black and beautiful.
She'd charmed him with a smile and before he knew
what had hit him, he'd been ushering her into his
place, pouring wine and spilling his guts about his
background while they waited for the locksmith.

She'd been smart—she'd made him laugh. He'd
adored her big brown eyes, her full mouth, the way
she absently touched him when she'd been reading
the paper. He'd been so damn sure she was the one.

While he might have recovered from the relationship, the pain of her betrayal still cut through him like
fire. Why hadn't he been able to see through her fa-
cade? He'd always thought he was so clever about

people—at the department he'd had a reputation for cutting to the heart of someone's motive. But he hadn't sensed anything amiss with Sylvia. Not even for a second.

He'd felt so angry, so betrayed. He'd refused her requests that they talk one more time. Before Mark had left New York, her attorney had tried to give Mark a letter from Sylvia. Mark had torn it into pieces and handed it back to the attorney with instructions that Sylvia never contact him again.

She hadn't. There had been silence, and now she was gone.

Mark leaned back in his chair and closed his eyes. Guilt hovered, but he shoved it away. *He* hadn't done anything wrong. So why did he feel as if he'd been emotionally skinned alive?

He rose to his feet and headed for the parking lot. The need to keep moving nearly pushed him to a run. One day Sylvia had been his whole world and the next he'd been in the hospital, fighting for his life. He'd walked away from her without looking back, but always with the expectation he would have to face her again. Now that wouldn't happen.

When he reached his truck, he unlocked the door and slipped inside. He'd told himself he'd done a good job of letting her go. It had been a whole lot easier than he would have thought, which made him question whether or not he'd ever loved her. If he had, he was an idiot. If he hadn't, he'd never loved anyone. He didn't like either option. Maybe the truth was something else entirely. Maybe he'd simply allowed himself to forget because it was easier than remembering.

He drove without thinking and found himself at home. An acid rawness burned at his soul. He didn't want to be alone. Not with the pain or the ghosts. He stared at the apartment building. Two halves of a whole, he thought numbly. Solitude or solace. It wasn't a difficult choice.

Instead of leaving his truck and walking toward his front door, he headed to Darcy's side of the building and knocked. He didn't bother to analyze why he was here, because he already knew. She was his neighbor and a woman with secrets—could there be a worse combination? Yet there wasn't anyone else he wanted to speak with at that moment. No one else he wanted to see. She was the kind of woman who rescued by instinct and right now he was in some serious need of saving.

She opened the door. Instantly the scent of gingerbread drifted out to greet him. Darcy smiled. There was flour on her cheek and sweater. Her sleeves were pulled up to her elbows, her hair tucked back behind her ears.

"Hi, Mark, what's up?" Her smile faded as she studied him. "I mean this in the nicest possible way, but you look awful. What's wrong?"

She stepped back and he entered her house.

"Someone I know is dead," he said abruptly. "A suicide."

Darcy sucked in her breath at the news. "I'm so sorry."

He stared into her eyes. Compassion overruled

shock. He shouldn't have come, he realized. She didn't need this particular brand of hell screwing up her life.

But he couldn't force himself to leave.

"I don't know what I feel," he admitted. "Anger. Relief. Maybe guilt. I don't know. How am I supposed to get closure? How will this ever be okay?" He shook his head. "It won't be. I guess that's the point."

"You're in shock," she said softly. "The mourning will come later and, with it, clarity. As for closure, time is a great healer."

"I don't think so. I don't think it's going to be that easy."

"Oh, it's not easy. Letting go and forgiving are the hardest things in the world."

"I don't want to forgive. Maybe there's something wrong with me. I can't feel hurt or anger or even compassion. Maybe I'm incapable of feeling anything significant. Maybe—"

She stepped close and put her arms around him. "Can you feel that?" she asked.

He held himself completely still. The warmth of her body chased away a chill he hadn't known was there. Her breasts flattened against his chest, while her legs brushed against his. Her hair smelled like vanilla.

Desire slammed into him. He might not be able to mourn Sylvia's passing, but he sure could want Darcy. His arousal was instant and nearly painful. Hunger heated his blood until the need to be with her was as compelling and instinctive as drawing in a breath.

Gathering all his strength, he gently untangled her arms from around him and moved away.

"I shouldn't have come here," he told her. "You don't need the complication and I can't be what you want me to be. I'm sorry." He headed for the door.

"Mark? I don't understand."

He turned back to her, glaring. "I'm not feeling especially friendly right now. I want more. Specifically you." He ran his fingers through his hair and swore. "I shouldn't have come here," he repeated. "I don't know why I did. I'm sorry."

He reached for the door handle.

"Wait," she called before he could leave. "Just wait."

He froze in place. The sensible part of him, the part that knew he was more than capable of hurting Darcy, told him to keep on walking. If he cared at all about her, he wouldn't be with her now—like this. But the rawness inside of him was stronger. It kept him in place as she turned off the oven and returned to his side. When she took his hand he didn't protest. When she led him into her bedroom, he reached for her.

Mark's intense kiss made her burn down to her toes. Darcy clung to him, her own passion flaring in the face of his obvious need. If he'd tried to seduce her, she thought she might have been able to be strong, although maybe not. But his pain, the lost look in his eyes, the way he'd come to her first, had all conspired to make her unable to resist him.

His mouth brushed frantically against hers. She parted for him and he plunged into her, tasting her, tempting her to do the same to him. His hands moved restlessly, rubbing up and down her back, drawing her closer until she pressed against him so tightly she thought she might merge with him and become one.

His need made her want him more. She clung to him as their world began to spin slowly. She touched his face, his shoulders, felt the cool, silky strands of his hair. His chest rose and fell with each labored breath. She felt herself surrendering without a single thought to what this all could mean to her heart.

When he tugged at her sweater, she raised her arms. He pulled off that garment. As he shrugged out of his own shirt, she kicked off her shoes and removed her socks. Before she could take off anything else, he reached for her bra and unfastened the hooks.

His mouth was on her in an instant, sucking her already tight nipples, licking them, making her gasp and beg him never to stop. He cupped her breasts, using his fingers to match the movements of his tongue. She rubbed his bare back, digging into the flexing muscles there, murmuring his name, wishing she had the will to stop him, yet knowing she wouldn't even if she could.

He dropped to his knees and opened the fastening of her jeans. He pulled down the denim, along with her panties, then supported her while she stepped out of her clothes. Clasping the curve of her hips, he bent forward and kissed her between her thighs. He touched her most private place with the tip of his tongue, promising her much, while teasing her with the lightest of contacts. She sucked in her breath.

Without saying a word, he rose and led her to the

bed. At his urging, she lay on her stomach, her head cradled in her arms.

"Protection?" he asked quietly, whispering the single word in her ear. She shivered as his warm breath tickled her skin.

A little embarrassed at her own boldness, she pointed at the nightstand drawer.

"I bought some a couple of days ago."

He knelt beside her and licked the sensitive skin just below her ear. "I thought we were only going to be friends. Or were they not meant for me?"

She gave a strangled laugh, torn between listening to what he was saying and the nibbling sensation on the lobe of her ear.

"I, ah, thought I might have a moment of weakness. I didn't want to be unprepared. And with the weather as cold as it is, I didn't think you'd want to be running back to your place."

"What kind did you get?"

"Extra large."

He chuckled, then grew quiet. One of his hands settled on her rear. He rubbed her skin, circling across to her opposite hip before returning. She felt a puff of breath as her only warning before he bent down and lightly bit the skin on her side.

As he nibbled his way up and down her back she felt herself growing more and more ready. Then he shifted and bit down firmly on her rear, making her shriek.

"Mark! What are you doing?"

"Nothing."

He moved lower, licking his way down her thighs

to her knees. His ministrations began to tickle. She squirmed, trying to get away without accidentally kicking him. He held her in place, licking the inside of her knees.

Darcy finally managed to break free and turn onto her back.

"Better," he said, returning his attention to her legs, but this time on the front.

Tension tightened her belly. Her thighs began to tremble. He licked his way up to her tender, willing femininity, then kissed her there. She sank back on the bed, grateful for both his skillful touch and the fact that the shadows had faded from his eyes. She wanted to think about what he'd told her, but she couldn't—not with him licking her center and making her breath come in ragged pants.

He slipped one finger inside of her, teasing the place that would soon welcome him. His tongue touched her from above, his finger from below. Both moved in tandem until she knew her release was inevitable as the tide.

"Mark! Please...I want to finish with you inside of me."

"You will," he murmured against her. "The second time."

She wanted to protest. She wanted to pull him so that he was forced to enter her, filling her, stretching her until she had no choice but to surrender.

The erotic image was a mistake. As the fantasy fully formed, she lost control and slipped over the edge into the glory of her release. Her body arched toward him, carrying her to paradise.

She quivered and gasped until the last whisper of her climax had faded. It was only then that he shifted, swinging his legs over the side of the bed and pulling off his jeans and briefs. He leaned toward the nightstand, pulled open the drawer and removed a condom. When he was protected, he knelt between her thighs.

For a long time he didn't move. He simply stared at her, studying her face as if memorizing every feature. Darcy didn't mind the attention—there was a kind expression in his eyes and she didn't think he would find her wanting. Finally he leaned close and kissed her neck. He moved lower until he could caress her breasts.

A familiar heat filled her. She reached for him, running her fingers up and down his back. As her desire grew, she became more insistent, pressing on the small of his back, urging him closer.

Finally he entered her. Slowly...so slowly...making her call out for him to hurry, then catching her breath when he finally found his way home. Once there, he began to move more quickly. His thrusts became frantic. He supported himself on his hands and gazed into her eyes.

She felt herself readying for another climax. With him looking at her so intently, she felt exposed. Yet she couldn't seem to close her eyes. Even as the first spasms swept through her, she stared into his soul. Perhaps this act would heal him.

He stiffened. His expression tightened. Still he didn't look away. They climaxed together, still staring at each other. The act of intimacy somehow became more of a connection than she'd experienced before.

When Mark finally sank down on the bed and pulled her close, Darcy felt shaken.

Something had fundamentally changed between them. She didn't understand what, but the possibilities frightened her. Wanting to heal him was one thing— she was good at doing that. But engaging her heart was quite another. Not only did she sense that Mark wasn't a man looking for a relationship, there was still the issue of the secrets of her past.

"Thank you," he breathed against her hair.

"You're welcome."

They held each other in silence. Finally he kissed her mouth.

"Are you going to ask me about today?"

She knew he wasn't talking about the fact that they'd made love. Instead he meant the suicide of someone he had known.

"Do you think talking will help you?"

"No, but you have the right to get some answers."

Rights given to her by virtue of them both being naked. Darcy sighed. Those kinds of rights were often complicated.

"Was he a close friend?"

Mark stiffened. In that second, Darcy knew she'd asked the wrong questions. She instantly felt stupid and used. The suicide hadn't been by a male friend. No, a woman had died. Someone significant to Mark.

"Never mind," she said quickly.

He winced. "Darcy, I'm sorry. I thought I'd said 'she.' I wasn't trying to keep that from you."

Every cell in her body screamed at her to cover herself and run. But that would mean letting him know that he'd hurt her, and for some reason she wasn't willing to expose herself that way.

"I know you weren't trying to be sly. It doesn't matter."

She sat up and gave him a big smile. What she wanted to do instead was cry, but she was determined to keep her emotions to herself.

"On second thought, questions are probably a mistake," she said with a brightness she didn't feel. "We're friends. That's what matters. I want to be here for you." Although maybe next time it would be better if the "here" didn't include her bed.

"I'm sorry," he repeated.

Not "she didn't matter." Darcy told herself she was overreacting. It wasn't reasonable to expect Mark to have not had a life before meeting her. Which made logical sense but didn't explain the tears burning in her eyes. She couldn't justify the tears...or maybe she could. Maybe they came from the unexpected heaviness in her heart.

"Morning," Mark said as he slid into his usual booth at the Hip Hop.

Darcy poured him a cup of coffee. It was Wednesday and the café was just starting to empty out.

"Someone is late," she teased, the light tone a part of her plan to act completely normal.

"I overslept."

She studied the dark circles under his green eyes. "Looks like you didn't sleep at all."

"I did great from about five until seven this morning."

She thought about asking what was wrong, but she had a feeling she knew. His lady friend. That's how she'd come to think of the woman who had killed herself over the weekend.

At first Darcy had tried to convince herself they were just friends, but Mark's reaction had been all wrong for that. He'd come to her house because he'd needed close, physical contact. The loss of a friend required a hug. The loss of a lover needed much more.

Darcy told herself it wasn't her business. Mark's past was his problem. It's not as if she expected him to have been a virgin the first time they'd done it. When he'd come calling on Sunday she could have told him no. But she hadn't. She'd wanted to take away his pain—if only for the moment—and making love had been the only thing she could think of to do.

The thing was, she wasn't sure she would have reacted the same way if she'd known the person in question had been a woman.

She didn't think Mark had kept the information from her deliberately, but the knowledge had changed everything. Unfortunately, their shift in relationship had left her unsure of what was going to happen next.

He studied her carefully. "You don't look like you've been sleeping much, either. Any of that have something to do with me?"

"No. I'm fine," she told him, hating that his concern made her go all gooey inside.

"Really?"

"I swear."

He didn't bother picking up the menu she'd placed in front of him. "Then I'll have the usual."

"I don't think so."

He nearly smiled. "We've had this discussion before and I always win."

"Not this time. I'm tired of you trying to eat yourself into an early grave. One day this week you're going to have oatmeal for breakfast. I don't care what day and I especially don't care if you try to refuse. It's gonna happen. Now we can do this the easy way or the hard way. It's up to you."

She expected an argument, but Mark surprised her by leaning back in the booth and agreeing.

"Why not?" he asked. "I might as well get it over with, so I'll have oatmeal today."

She was shocked enough not to do much more than blink at him for a full minute.

"Darcy?" He waved his hand in front of her face. "Earth to Darcy."

"Does this mean you're going to have a salad for lunch instead of a burger?"

"Don't push it."

"A girl can dream."

She regretted the choice of words as soon as they passed her lips. Rather than try to explain she hadn't meant anything by them, she gave him a quick smile and disappeared toward the kitchen to write up his order.

Five minutes later she was back with a bowl of oatmeal, a small pitcher of two percent milk, brown sugar and raisins.

He gazed at his meal as if she'd offered him stir-fried bugs. "Does it have to be so gray?"

"It's not gray, it's kind of ecru."

"And that's more appealing how?"

His words were light, but she could still see the lingering pain in his eyes.

"*You* all right, Mark?" she asked, turning the tables and studying him.

"Sure. Fine." He glanced at her. "Okay, how about I'm putting it in perspective."

"That one I'll accept. I've been worried about you."

He raised one eyebrow. "Do you always try to save the world?"

"Not the world, just a few bits of it."

"How'd I get to be so lucky as to have you around just when I needed you?"

She studied him to see if he was being sarcastic, but she didn't think he was taunting her.

"We're friends," she said. "As for my desire to do the right thing—I have twenty years of being useless to make up for."

"You're wrong, Darcy. You were a kid for most of those twenty years. Your only responsibility was to grow up and I'd say you did a fine job of that."

His compliment pleased her. She excused herself to check on her other customers and tried not to think about Mark while she worked.

She knew she was attracted to the man. She didn't want it to be that way, but it was too late now not to notice him. Harder to ignore were the danger signs flashing in her brain. He was dangerous to her—she knew it with every fiber of her being. They hadn't made love since Sunday and not an hour went by that she didn't think about what they'd done and wish they were doing it again. Worse, she found herself missing him when they weren't together, which was most of the time.

"Don't do this to yourself," she murmured quietly as she cleared tables and pocketed the tips. "Don't get involved."

Unfortunately, she wasn't listening.

"How was it?" she asked when she returned to Mark's table.

He pointed at the near-empty bowl. "I didn't gag, but I don't want it every day."

"Studies show that—"

He winced. "Spare me, please."

"Okay. Just this once. By the way there's going to be a great chicken-vegetable salad on the menu for lunch."

He ignored her comment. "There's a craft fair on Saturday. I thought you might like to go."

Her stomach turned over. Was he asking her as a friend or as something more? They had not redefined their relationship since last Sunday and she was afraid to bring it up now...mostly because she wasn't sure what she wanted his answer to be.

"I wouldn't have thought you were the craft-fair type," she said. "Won't all those knickknacks and homemade goodies give you hives?"

"I thought you'd have fun."

His green eyes were so beautiful, she thought suddenly. She could very happily drown in them. Which only showed she was losing her mind.

"I can't," she said regretfully. "I already have plans."

"Anyone I know?"

It was a casual enough question. She searched for an edge to his voice—maybe a hint of jealousy. She didn't find any.

"Nope. Just some stuff I need to do."

Actually, she was going to visit Dirk and hear all about his trip, but Mark didn't need to know that. At least not yet. At some point in time she was going to have to tell him the truth. Tell him and watch him walk out the door.

"Maybe next time," he said, putting several bills on the table.

"I'd like that."

As he left, she wondered how much longer they would have as friends or whatever it was that explained their relationship. And how much she would miss him when he was gone.

Mark drove slowly through town searching for a beat-up dark green import. There wasn't a single one in sight. Whatever Darcy's plans had been for the day, they'd taken her out of town.

He circled through the main section of Whitehorn again, but couldn't spot anyone who looked the least bit like his blond neighbor.

He turned around and headed for home. As he drove, he told himself it didn't matter that she'd had other plans for the day. He hadn't really wanted to see her. Or had he? What exactly had happened between them the previous Sunday when he'd found out about Sylvia's suicide?

It hadn't just been sex. He wanted the intimacy between them to have had no meaning, but he didn't believe that was true. Something about Darcy healed his soul the same way the doctors had healed his body. He found himself thinking about her at odd times during the day and wanting to be with her again. In his bed, her bed, the shower, he didn't much care as long as they were both naked.

Worse, he felt badly for hurting her. He should never have involved her in the horror of his past. Darcy deserved better than that.

Was he entering into dangerous territory? He knew better than to care about anyone. More important, he knew better than to trust again. Darcy had her secrets. Her absence today proved that. Telling himself her life wasn't any of his business didn't change the fact that he still wanted to know where the hell she'd gone.

Chapter Eight

Sunday afternoon Mark settled in front of his desk, determined to catch up on paperwork. He wasn't going to think about anything but the cases he'd cleared and what he was going to do to finish up the forms required to send everything to wherever it belonged. He wasn't going to spend a single second thinking about Darcy.

So what if she hadn't showed up for his weekly basketball game? He hadn't invited her. They didn't have an understanding. They weren't even dating. They were friends—friends and sometime lovers. That kind of relationship didn't require an explanation of one's time. Even when she hadn't arrived home until 10:05 the previous evening.

He opened the top file on his desk and reached for his computer keyboard. As he entered the necessary information, Darcy slowly faded from his mind until he was able to fully concentrate on his work. Two hours later, he'd cleared three cases and was working on a fourth when he heard footsteps in the empty office. He looked up and saw Sheriff Rafe Rawlings walking toward him. They were about the same age. Tall with dark hair, Rafe was well respected in town.

Mark leaned back in his chair. "What are you doing here? Someone try to rob a bank on a Sunday?"

Rafe grinned. "Not on my watch. They wouldn't dare." He pulled up a chair and settled into it. "I tried you at home a couple of times this morning. When you didn't pick up, I figured you might be here."

Mark noticed his boss's worried expression. "Want to talk about it?"

Rafe shrugged. "I got a tip the other day. It was so crazy that I couldn't believe it. I did a little checking on my own, but I can't come up with anything. It's probably nothing...."

Rafe's voice trailed off. Mark stiffened. He had a bad feeling about whatever the sheriff was going to say.

"You ready to hand it over to a professional," he quipped, trying to keep things light.

"That I am." Rafe leaned forward. "I received an anonymous tip that someone is running a money-laundering operation out of the Hip Hop Café."

Mark's first reaction was disbelief. This was Whitehorn. Nothing very interesting happened here. However, that wasn't always true and bad money had a way of turning up in the most unassuming places.

"Where did you start?" he asked.

"You're not dismissing the tip."

"Better to investigate and prove it wrong than to do nothing and have it come back to bite us in the butt later."

"I agree," Rafe said. "I asked around some, but I didn't find anything."

"You talk to any of the employees?" Mark asked, hating that the first person who came to mind was Darcy. Although she'd done nothing to make him think she was anything but a law-abiding citizen, his experience with Sylvia had forever changed how he looked at any woman he knew.

"I had a few words with Janie Carson Austin. She's lived here all her life and I can vouch for her myself. I didn't tell her much because I realized you should be the one getting into it, not me. As you said, you're the pro."

"That's why you hired me." Mark reached for a pad of paper. "I'll be checking into everyone. Even Janie, which is strange because we went to high school together. Still, people change." Though in Janie's case, he doubted she'd taken up a life of crime.

"Do what you have to. I suggest you clear her first, so you can use her for a point of contact. Are you friendly with any of the staff there?"

"I know a few of them." One in particular, but he didn't say that.

Rafe gave him a few more instructions, then left. Mark stared after his boss, wishing this hadn't come up now.

He knew he could do a good job investigating—he was just apprehensive about what he would find out about Darcy. Reminding himself that she lived modestly and worked long hours didn't make him feel any better. He'd trusted Sylvia and look how that had turned out.

He scribbled some notes to himself, then turned to his computer. Unable to stop himself, he typed in a single name.

Darcy Montague.

Mark waited until Darcy finished her shift on Monday before heading over to the Hip Hop. Which meant he missed his usual breakfast. He'd spent the previous afternoon and most of the night on the computer clearing Janie, which was why he was here. He was hungry, tired and as crabby as a bear in spring.

He walked into the café close to three. There were only two customers. The waitress on duty said that Janie was in her office in the back. Mark made his way to the cramped space and knocked on the open door.

Janie looked up and smiled. "Howdy, stranger. I didn't think you were speaking to me these days."

"I'm talking."

"Not to most of us. Since you've been home, you haven't been the least bit neighborly."

He sat down in the only spare chair in her office. "Sorry about that, Janie. I've had a lot on my mind."

Her smile faded. "I guess getting shot would give a man something to think about."

He studied her pretty features. He and Janie were

the same age; he'd known her most of his life. In the eighth grade he'd thought she was as pretty as an angel and it had taken him two years to get over his crush on her. All these years later she was happily married and he felt as old as the black hills.

"Something's come up," he said.

She nodded. "The sheriff was in here a couple of days ago asking me a lot of questions. I got the feeling there was a problem. Want to talk to me about it?"

"Actually I want to talk to you about the people who work for you. We've had a tip that someone is laundering money here at the Hip Hop."

Janie's blue eyes widened as her mouth gaped open. "You're not serious."

"I'm afraid I am."

"There's not enough money going through this place. I mean, we do well for a restaurant in Whitehorn, but it's not as if this is Chicago and we're talking about thousands flowing through here every day."

"There are more ways to launder money than through the cash register. Although I wouldn't be surprised if the sheriff brings in someone to go over the books."

Her gaze narrowed. "Because you're going to recommend it?"

"It's part of my job."

She threw up her hands. "Mark, I don't know anything about this, but I want to cooperate with you. The sooner you start investigating, the sooner you'll find out that someone was playing a joke on you and Rafe."

"I hope so. I'd like to see a list of employees."

Janie typed on the computer, then hit the print button. Seconds later a single sheet of paper appeared. He took it and glanced at the names. Darcy's was on it, but then she worked here.

"Thanks. I'm going to be checking into the backgrounds of the employees. Anything you want to tell me now?"

"No. I'm not aware of anyone having a criminal record. At least nothing anyone has told me about. I've known some of these people for years."

"And some are new."

She frowned and took the list from him. "Darcy is our most recent hire. She's been here about six months." She returned her attention to him. "Mark, I refuse to believe she's doing anything illegal. You know her—you two are neighbors. The woman works her butt off all day here, then heads home to bake for several local businesses."

"I have to check out everyone."

She pressed her lips together. "Don't get all gung ho about this. If you go tearing in like you're trying to beat the clock, you may end up ruining what looks to be a very promising relationship."

He wondered what Darcy had told Janie about them. Were the two women close? "I appreciate the advice."

"Yeah, right. But the truth is you're going to do exactly what you want. Just don't forget, Darcy is a born caretaker with a big heart. She's sweet and kind and if you hurt her, I'll be really pissed off."

"Point taken. Tell me about the other employees."

Janie took him down the list, telling him what she knew about each individual. He made notes, wrote down addresses and phone numbers, all the while asking questions.

"Are you going to talk to Melissa?" Janie asked.

Mark nodded. He still had to check out Melissa North, the owner of the Hip Hop Café.

"You know she's out of town," Janie said. "On a second honeymoon. I'd really hate to interrupt her vacation."

"No point right now. If that changes and I need to talk to her before she's due back, I'll let you know."

"Okay." She tilted her head. "I sure hope I don't get that call."

"I hope I don't have to make it." He rose to his feet. "Janie, I need you to keep quiet about this. Please don't discuss this with anyone."

"I figured that one out on my own. You'll keep me informed, won't you?"

"As much as I can without compromising the investigation."

She stood. "I would never want your job. I'd hate knowing the worst about people."

He nodded. Sometimes he didn't like it, either.

He headed to his truck. Once he was back at the office, he would investigate each of the employees. And he would take a second run at Darcy. So far he'd turned up exactly nothing. She didn't even have a parking ticket. Was she really that good, or was her history planted?

He tried telling himself she wasn't anything like

Sylvia, but how was he ever supposed to let the past go enough to trust anyone again?

Mark headed over to Darcy's place around seven that evening. He'd put it off as long as he could, but eventually he was going to have to speak with her. He might as well get it over with.

She called, "Come in," when he knocked.

He pushed open the front door and stepped into her living room.

"I could be a serial killer," he said as he headed for the kitchen.

She looked up from where she stood at the counter. "I don't have any cereal in the house. I eat oatmeal every day."

He groaned. "Why am I not surprised?"

As he stepped into the kitchen, he found that he very much wanted to move close and kiss her. Not a deep passionate kiss, although he wouldn't mind that, but a greeting kind of kiss. One that said "hello" and "how was your day?" He missed her and how he felt when he was around her.

The realization made him swear under his breath. He had to keep his distance from this woman, both physically and emotionally.

Darcy returned her attention to her work. He saw that she'd baked Christmas cookies and was decorating them. As he watched, she piped red frosting onto a Santa cookie, filling in the coat.

"Don't get all huffy about the front door," she said without looking up. "I usually keep it locked, but I knew I'd be in here baking and I hoped you'd stop by. I didn't see you at the Hip Hop this morning.''

"I was tied up at work.''

"Oh.''

She kept the single word response neutral so he couldn't tell what she was thinking.

"I'm glad it was just work,'' she continued. "I was getting a little worried. I thought you might be sick or something.''

"I don't need rescuing.''

He spoke more sharply than he'd intended. She flinched slightly. A drop of frosting slipped onto the counter.

"Obviously not,'' she murmured.

He swore under his breath. "Darcy, it's not that. I just…''

He just what? Wanted her to tell him that she'd never done anything illegal in her life? Or say that she wasn't like Sylvia? That it was safe for him to sleep with her because she wasn't going to try and hold him, but instead would freely let him go when he needed to run?

He knew he was being a jerk. Some of it was the investigation, some of it was his past. He couldn't help wondering if he had any responsibility in Sylvia's suicide. Telling himself he didn't hadn't erased the questions.

Was he screwing up Darcy's life by getting involved with her? Was he willing to walk away?

She finished with the first Santa and moved on to a second. There were already a couple of dozen cookies drying on racks on the kitchen counter. Santas and green trees with tiny ornaments, stars and candy canes. She worked quickly, with an ease that came with long practice. The overhead light turned the tips of her blond hair to gold. Her eyelashes cast shadows on her cheeks.

"Do you make cookies every year?" he asked.

"Sure. Some I give away. I'm taking a few dozen over to the hospital tomorrow for the kids and the staff. I'll be selling some through the Hip Hop. I really enjoy holiday baking."

He hated what he was doing, but he couldn't stop himself. He crossed to the table and pulled out a chair. Right now he needed answers more than he needed to be her friend. No way would he admit that he just might be using the case to keep his emotional distance.

"It must be nice to have a white Christmas after all those years in Arizona."

She glanced out the window. Snow fell steadily. They were due to get a couple of inches that night. Humor brightened her eyes.

"I agree that the snow is picturesque, but there are times I really miss the heat. I'm sure that come mid-January I'll be wishing I was back in the desert."

He itched to pull out his pad and start taking notes. "Is that why you moved from Illinois to Arizona in the first place? To get away from the winter?"

He hated that she looked away before answering.

"Some of it. Also, I'd just lost my parents and I wanted a change."

"I'm surprised you didn't want to stay where everything was familiar. Starting over isn't easy."

"I see your point, but it was different for me. None of my so-called friends had stayed by me. I didn't think I was giving anything up by moving on."

The argument sounded convincing, but her body language and his gut told him otherwise.

"What brought you back to the Midwest? And why Montana?"

Darcy carefully finished the last Santa coat, then switched to white icing. As she piped on trim, she nibbled on her bottom lip.

"It was time to try somewhere new," she said at last. "As for Montana, I don't know. I'd heard so much about it. There's a lot of natural beauty here—outdoor sports, that sort of thing."

He doubted she could get a pair of skis into her car, and she didn't have a roof rack. Besides, Darcy didn't strike him as the sports type. When would she find the time? Between her full-time job at the Hip Hop and her baking, she seemed to keep herself busy.

"Why all the questions?" she asked softly.

Now it was his turn to look away. "No reason."

"I think there might be. You didn't come into the café today. Are you avoiding me, Mark?"

"There's a new case. I can't talk about it."

She accepted his explanation with a nod. Either she didn't notice he hadn't answered her question, or she wasn't going to push it.

"What about your friend's death? I'm sure you're not over that."

He grimaced. "Sylvia wasn't a friend."

"I think you two were very close."

Darcy's comment invited confession, but he wasn't in the mood to admit he'd made such a big mistake.

He stood up and paced the length of the kitchen. Restlessness filled him. He wanted Darcy. Even as he questioned her, his body tightened in anticipation. Only they weren't going to be making love today. Probably not anytime soon, if ever again. Not while he wasn't sure about her.

What was he doing here? He should either ask her some pointed questions or get the hell out of her place. But asking questions meant hearing answers and he didn't know if he was ready for that.

He hated the darkness inside his soul. Life had been a whole lot easier when he hadn't worried about anyone but himself.

"I know what you need," Darcy said in a bright tone that sounded forced. "Sugar and caffeine. Go sit in the living room and I'll bring in some cookies and coffee."

"No, I don't want to eat your cookies. You're going to sell them to the Hip Hop."

"I'll be giving a bunch away to the hospital, as well, so don't worry about eating up my business. Besides, you really look like you need a cookie."

Her blue eyes were large and innocent. She couldn't know how much he wanted that innocence to be true.

"Okay. Cookies and coffee sound great."

He walked into the living room, but instead of taking a seat, he prowled around.

"Do you really want coffee?" Darcy called from

the kitchen. "It's kinda late. What about milk instead."

"Either," he said.

On the mantel there was a picture of young girl with an attractive, well-dressed couple. He assumed it was of Darcy and her parents. Next to that was a small plant of some kind, and a pink and white box. He raised the lid, expecting to hear music. There was only silence...and the sound of his heart.

Mark stared at the folded bills neatly placed in the small box. The thick wad of money seemed to be mostly fifties. There had to be at least a couple of thousand dollars here. In cash.

He closed his eyes briefly, not wanting it to be her. Not Darcy. He wanted to find another reason for the money to be there. But the tips at the Hip Hop couldn't be that good, and Darcy hadn't been in town long enough for her business to take off. She didn't even have a contract with the Hip Hop.

He slammed the top on the box and forced himself to sit on the sofa. There had to be another explanation. He refused to believe that Darcy was involved in money laundering.

She smiled as she walked into the living room. A plate of cookies took up most of the tray. Two glasses of milk nestled together. She set the tray on the coffee table and settled next to him on the sofa.

"These are my favorites," she said, picking up a cookie in the shape of a bell and nibbling on the edge. "Actually I like the icing more than the cookies, but I can't allow myself to sit down and eat just icing. So I choke down the cookie part, too."

She smiled as she spoke, an easy smile that made him wonder if he'd imagined the money. But he knew he hadn't. He felt betrayed for the second time. Something he'd never wanted to experience again.

Why did it matter if she was a criminal? He told himself he didn't care about Darcy. So maybe they'd been lovers a few times. They might have even started to be friends, but so what?

He stood suddenly. "I have to go."

Darcy stared after Mark. One second they'd been sitting together talking and the next, he'd been gone. What had happened? She put down the cookie she'd been eating. It seemed that her run of bad luck with men was endless.

She didn't know why Mark had left, but she had figured out that something was very wrong. Despite his claims to the contrary, he'd been avoiding her. What she didn't know was why. Had he found out about Dirk? Mark had sure been in detective mode with all his questions. Obviously he suspected something, but what? How could he have found out about the school and her brother's challenges?

Did it matter? She slumped back on the sofa. For a while she'd thought that Mark's time in caring for his sister might have made him more understanding and accepting of her situation. Obviously she'd been wrong about that, and him. He thought she was good enough to sleep with, but not good enough for anything else.

"The hell with him," she said aloud. But her voice was a whisper, and she was having a hard time ignoring the tears pooling in her eyes.

Chapter Nine

Darcy knocked on the counseling office door. Andrew looked up and waved her in.

"I didn't expect to see you until the weekend," he said.

She took the seat opposite his. "I just wanted to drop by and say hi to Dirk."

Andrew raised his eyebrows. "We're fifty miles from Whitehorn on a two-lane farm road, Darcy. Is there a problem?"

"No. Really. I'm fine. How's Dirk?"

"Making great progress." Andrew leaned back in his chair. "Some things are easier for him to grasp than others. You know our goal here is help our students be as self-sufficient as possible in the real world. Dirk will never be a CEO of a major company but, as I told you when he first arrived, I think there are a lot of opportunities for him. Now that I've worked with him for six months, I don't see any reason to change my opinion. If anything, I'm more confident.''

''Thanks.'' She fidgeted with the strap of her purse. ''I'm still going to be able to make monthly payments, right?''

''Absolutely.'' Andrew chuckled. ''Actually, you've caught me in the middle of putting together a financial-aid package for you. Now that Dirk has been here long enough for us to evaluate him, we're going to start the process of applying for scholarship and grant money.''

''You can do that?'' she asked, not daring to hope.

''We can try. We don't talk about it as an option when we get a new student because there are restrictions. One of them is how much the student can be helped. Our belief is that Dirk will be about ninety percent self-sufficient by the time he leaves here. He'll be able to hold down a job, live on his own and, within reason, support himself. That and the fact that he doesn't have any financial resources makes him eligible.''

Darcy bristled. ''I pay for things. I've never been late with a tuition payment.''

''Hey, don't make me the bad guy. The foundations we work with don't consider you a primary source of income. You're a sibling, not a parent. This is a good thing. It makes Dirk more eligible for funding.''

''Oh.'' She considered the information. ''I'm not going to start planning a trip to Hawaii or anything, but if we could get some financial aid, it would really help."

Andrew nodded, his expression turning serious. "I know you're hanging on by a thread, Darcy. Don't give up. I'm guessing within six months, we'll have funding for at least three-quarters of his tuition."

"That would be terrific," she admitted. "Some months it's difficult to pay all my bills." If the funding came through she might actually be able to save money for an emergency.

"We're not cheap," Andrew admitted. "I like to think we're worth it." He leaned forward, resting his elbows on the desk. "What else is wrong, Darcy? You don't seem to be your normal, cheerful self today."

She shrugged. "Just life. You know—there's always something."

"I'm a professional. I'm willing to listen."

"That sounds really tempting, but you're Dirk's counselor, not mine."

"I'd like to think we're friends. Talk to me."

She hesitated. "I don't know. There's this guy."

"Ah. A matter of the heart. I should have known."

"I don't know if this qualifies as a 'matter of the heart.' More like a confusing situation between people who are friends."

And lovers, but she wasn't comfortable confessing that. "He lives next door. We've hung out a few times." Did sex qualify as hanging out? "I thought we were getting along great, but last Monday he turned weird on me. I don't know. He mentioned some big case at work, but I'm not sure I believe him.''

''What kind of work does he do?''

''He's a detective. He worked in New York for a while, but he was injured on the job. I guess he left to recover and now he's here. He grew up in Whitehorn.''

''Sounds like he's made a lot of adjustments. First to the big city and now to coming home. How long has he been back?''

''A few months. I think a suspect shot him.''

Andrew frowned. ''That can't have been easy. Do you know any of the details of the shooting?''

''No. Just that he was in the hospital for a while and then in rehab.'' She thought about the scars on his body. ''One gunshot was to his thigh, the other his torso. I know that no major organs were hit, but I think it was pretty close.''

''Facing one's mortality is never easy. Especially if his injuries were serious enough to cause him to leave his job.''

Darcy considered Andrew's statement. She hadn't thought about the reasons for Mark's return to Whitehorn. ''I don't know if he came back because he couldn't physically do the job, or if it was something else.''

''Neither is going to make him feel good about himself,'' Andrew told her. ''Men frequently define themselves by what they do. If your friend couldn't do the job he loved, he would need some time to get used to that reality. If he left because he didn't want to deal with the pressures anymore, then there are different things going on. Either way, he's in for an adjustment.''

"You're right. I had just sort of assumed that it was all about me—his being weird, I mean. Maybe it isn't. A friend of his killed herself a few days ago.''

Andrew whistled. "A former girlfriend?''

"I don't know. Maybe. Probably.'' She shifted uneasily. "Maybe I'm fooling myself, but I don't think he's lost the love of his life, yet there's something going on. It's hard to explain.''

"Suicide is difficult for those left behind,'' Andrew said. "Your friend is probably feeling a lot of conflicted emotions. Being in a new relationship is only going to add to his confusion and guilt. Try not to take it personally.'' He shook his head. "Unless all this is too much work and you'd rather pass. You don't have to get involved with this guy, Darcy.''

"It's not that.'' She didn't think Mark was too much trouble. "I guess so much has happened so fast that I'm having trouble keeping my equilibrium.'' She tried to smile and had a feeling she didn't do a good job. "I'm so used to guys taking off the second they find out about Dirk. All this stuff with Mark isn't about that.''

"It's tough to find out we're not the center of the universe,'' he teased, then sobered. "Are you okay, Darcy? You're dealing with a lot right now.''

"I'm fine.'' At least she was trying to maintain some semblance of normal. Mark didn't make it easy.

Andrew leaned toward her. "Do you want to talk about Dirk's impact on your social life?''

"I'm not sure there's anything to say. It's not a

new story. I love my brother and I would do anything for him. One of the realities of the situation is that people—men especially—don't want to get involved if it's not going to be easy. Dirk isn't easy. There are emotional and financial commitments that will last a lifetime. At least if a woman has kids, the assumption is that the kids are going to grow up and be on their own eventually. That may not happen with Dirk.''

''I think it's a very good possibility with your brother,'' Andrew told her, ''but it's not a sure thing. As for the men you've met, I'm sorry they've all been so shallow. There are a few good ones out there and I suggest you keep on looking.''

''Oh, I haven't given up. I just have gotten more cautious.''

And foolish, she thought, as she remembered Mark. When he'd agreed to her request to be friends, she'd allowed herself to hope things might be different with him. Ironic that she couldn't blame his disappearance on Dirk.

''Keep looking, Darcy,'' Andrew said. ''You're a wonderful woman. Any man would be lucky to have you in his life.''

''Right. When you meet this paragon of virtue, be sure to give him my number, okay?''

''I promise.''

Darcy rose and left Andrew's office. As she entered the hallway, she tried to take comfort in his words—that Mark's problems might not be about her at all and that eventually she would meet someone who would see Dirk for the amazing young man he was. But the cheerful thoughts didn't brighten her mood.

Part of her didn't believe she was ever going to meet someone that farsighted. Part of her didn't want to meet anyone else.

She leaned against the wall and sighed. There was a truth she could have gone another few years without knowing. That she didn't want to meet Mr. Perfect. Instead she wanted Mark to be the man of her dreams. She wanted him to stop acting strange and fall in love with her. She wanted him to meet her brother and be okay with Dirk and what his special circumstances meant.

Darcy told herself to get real. Wishing for the moon was only a waste of time. She would be better off convincing herself that Mark was a jerk and that she should be happy he was out of her life. Unfortunately, she didn't believe that one, either.

"Hey Mark, where's the pretty lady with the cinnamon rolls?" Josh Anderson asked as Mark walked into the gym on Sunday morning.

"Busy."

"Too bad. She's a great cook." Josh eyed him speculatively. "Not bad looking, either."

Instead of answering, Mark grunted. If he were any kind of decent human being he would tell Josh that Darcy was indeed a great cook and very pretty. She was also smart, funny and incredible in bed. He grimaced. Okay, so he should probably keep that last bit to himself. But he could tell Josh the rest of it. After all, the thirty-something contractor was single. If Mark didn't want Darcy for himself...

He shrugged out of his jacket, then pulled off his

sweatpants and sweatshirt until he was down to shorts and a T-shirt. No way was he going to encourage Josh in the Darcy department. He tried telling himself it was because she was a suspect in a police investigation, but he knew that wasn't it at all. He might not want Darcy for himself, but he sure as hell didn't want any other guy sniffing around her.

The rest of the guys showed up and the game began. Mark found it difficult to keep his concentration on the ball and his teammates. Conversation flowed around him. He tried to participate, but a large part of his brain was too busy reminding him how long it had been since he'd last seen Darcy.

Nearly a week, he thought as Josh passed him the basketball. Mark headed for the far end of the court and tipped the ball into the net. He barely heard the calls of congratulations from his side and the boos from their opponents.

What was she thinking, he wondered. Had she noticed he hadn't been around? He shook his head as he realized that wasn't a fair question. Of course, she would have noticed. She wasn't Sylvia. Darcy didn't have an agenda. Although if she was laundering money, then the last thing she would want was to get involved with a detective. Unless she thought she could fool him. Which brought back too many uncomfortable memories.

A week. He hated that he missed her. Nearly as bad, he didn't feel comfortable going to the Hip Hop, so he'd been forced to actually cook a couple of meals. That had been a disaster.

"Heads up, Kincaid," someone called. A second later, the basketball slammed into his back.

Mark turned. Josh glared at him. "Are you playing or what?"

"Sorry." He took the ball out of bounds, then tossed it back into play.

He kept his concentration on the game for a few minutes. Then his thoughts once against drifted to Darcy. Had she realized that he hadn't been to the café? Did she wonder what had happened to their supposed friendship?

"I know what the problem is with Kincaid," one of the guys said. "Chick trouble. Darcy's not here. So you guys had a fight, right? What'd you do wrong?"

Josh grabbed the basketball. "What makes you think it's his fault?"

Nearly everyone laughed. "It's always the guy's fault."

Mark raised his hands in a gesture of surrender. "It was me and I don't want to talk about it."

He was joking but also telling the truth. Walking out on her without saying anything had been the coward's way out. He should have confronted her about the money. The thing was, he didn't want to know that she was involved. He'd spent most of the week investigating her, and he still couldn't link her to anything illegal. Which didn't mean a thing.

He stopped in the middle of the court and swore under his breath. He knew the next step. He would have to take his suspicions to Rafe and together they would get a search warrant for her place. As he couldn't explain the cash, there wasn't any other choice.

"Mark!"

Mark turned toward the sound of his name. As he moved, he felt his foot slip on a damp spot in the court. He scrambled to regain his balance, but it was too late. His ankle twisted painfully. His still-healing leg couldn't support his weight and he felt himself crashing to the ground. His last thought before his head connected with the wooden floor was that this was gonna hurt like hell.

Darcy carefully placed the template on the baked sheet of gingerbread. She'd already cut out the walls of the house. Once the roof was done, the pieces would need to cool a little more, then she would start assembling the two houses. She had all the candies she would need, but she was going to be a little short on the icing. After this was done, she would make a quick trip to the store to—

The phone rang.

She glanced up at the instrument, hating the sudden fluttering in her chest. There was no way Mark was phoning her. She hadn't seen the man in nearly a week. He'd disappeared from her life with no explanation and no warning. She was working through the stages of mourning just fine, thank you very much, although today she seemed to be stuck in anger.

The phone rang again. Reluctantly she put down her knife and picked up the receiver.

"Hello?"

"Hi, Darcy."

All the blood rushed from her head, forcing her to sink into a kitchen chair. She briefly closed her eyes and wished she didn't care that he had finally called her. How was she supposed to act? Happy? Angry? Hurt?

She settled on casual. "Mark. Nice to hear from you. How's it going?"

"Things have just gotten real interesting." He hesitated. "Are you mad that I haven't called?"

She sucked in a breath as annoyance filled her. "Not at all," she said through slightly clenched teeth. "I've been so busy getting ready for the holidays that I barely noticed. How's work?"

"I've been busy, too." There was a pause, then something that sounded oddly like a moan. "Darcy, the reason I'm calling is that I need a ride home."

Annoyance turned to fury. How dare he expect her to be at his beck and call after first running out on her with no explanation and then ignoring her?

"Mark, I'm in the middle of making a gingerbread house. This is a very delicate time in the process. I'm not sure I can get away."

"Okay. I understand. Josh is driving my car back to the duplex. I guess I'll page him to come get me here when he's done. I didn't mean to bother you."

She sighed, hating that she was wavering. "It's not a bother. Not exactly. Where are you?"

"The hospital. I wrenched my ankle. I slipped while I was playing basketball. The thing is, I can't drive for two days. Not until the swelling goes down."

He'd hurt himself. Nurturing instinct battled with

righteous indignation. It wasn't much of a contest. "I'll be right there," she said, and hung up the phone.

Twenty minutes later she walked into the emergency room of Whitehorn Memorial Hospital. The woman at the reception desk directed her to treatment room number three. Darcy stepped inside and saw Mark sitting on a hospital bed. His ankle was taped and elevated. There was also a huge bruise on the side of his face.

Her heart did a little fox-trot, her temper flared. It was an interesting combination, but then she'd always been torn where he was concerned.

Mark looked up and saw her. "Hi," he said, sounding sheepish. "I'm sorry to bother you."

"We're neighbors. I didn't mind helping." She moved closer to the bed and pointed at the swelling on his face. "You hit your head?"

"On the way down. I didn't lose consciousness and I don't have a concussion. It looks a lot worse than it is."

Darcy had the sudden desire to make it worse. Just as a payback. But she'd never been the violent type and wouldn't have a clue as to where to start.

He waved a piece of paper. "I have my instructions. Rest for twenty-four hours. Keep the ankle elevated, use ice. So I'm ready to go."

"All right. I'll go pull my car up to the entrance."

He pushed the call button for a nurse. "We'll meet you there."

Maneuvering Mark into her small car wasn't easy. His injured ankle banged against the door once and she was almost sorry for him. As they drove back to the duplex, she had a silent but heated conversation with herself during which she told him exactly what she thought of him. She was acerbic, pithy and completely cool. Unfortunately, she wasn't likely to be any of those things if she started talking out loud.

When they reached his place, he opened the door but waited before getting out.

"Thanks for taking the time to come get me," he said.

She nodded.

"I know you're busy with your holiday baking."

She nodded again.

He glared at her. "Aren't you going to talk to me?"

She turned to face him. "What do you want me to say? I came to get you because we're supposed to be friends and that's what friends do for each other. Although some people seem to define friendship by acting weird and then disappearing off the face of the planet."

He gave her a tentative smile. "Would you feel any better if I had actually been off the planet?"

She didn't respond to the twinkle of amusement in his gaze. "Were you off the planet? Did you involve yourself with space travel this week?"

His smile faded. "No."

"I thought not."

She got out of the car and came around to the passenger side. He swung himself around until he was facing the open car door, then pulled himself to his feet without putting any weight on the injured ankle.

She had to reach around him to grab the crutches he'd been given.

As she did so, her arm brushed against his side. Heat jumped between them, making her nervous as well as crabby. She hated that he could get to her without doing anything but standing in the snow, looking pathetic.

She pulled out the crutches. "I'll need your key to open the door."

He dug it out of his sweatpants and handed it to her. She was careful to make sure they didn't touch again.

His progress to his front door was slow, hampered by five or six inches of fresh snow on the ground. More was promised midweek. Darcy tried to admire the beauty of the white world around them, the way the snow clung to the trees and decorated the duplex like so much icing, rather than feeling badly for Mark as he made slow and awkward progress.

Finally they were inside. Darcy got him settled on the sofa, which apart from a television sitting on a nightstand, was the only piece of furniture in the room. She set the crutches on the floor, then asked him where he kept his spare blankets.

"I don't have any. There's one on the bed."

"Figures."

She headed for the small hallway. His apartment was the mirror image of hers. At least the layout was. Nothing about the interior was the same. The walls looked as if they hadn't been painted in years. There weren't any pictures on the walls, and when she reached the bedroom, she saw he filled the room with a king-size bed, one nightstand and a tall dresser. Nothing else. Nothing personal.

Some of her anger began to fade in the face of his empty life. Why did Mark choose to live like this? Her apartment had been old when she'd moved in, but she'd painted the walls and dressed things up with inexpensive prints and knickknacks she'd brought from Arizona. She'd wanted to make a home for herself. Mark's place had all the charm of a prison. Did he expect to be moving on soon?

She collected the down comforter from the unmade bed, along with two pillows. Back in the living room, she slipped the pillows under his injured leg.

"Should you ice it?" she asked.

"Not for a couple more hours." He took the comforter from her. "Darcy, you don't have to do this. I can take care of myself."

"Sure." She avoided his gaze. "Have you eaten?"

"I'll be fine."

She forced herself to look at him. The bruise on his face looked really painful. "That wasn't the question."

"No. I haven't."

She turned on her heel and headed for the kitchen. It was a dreadful shade of green. There weren't any dishes in sight. On a hunch, she opened a cupboard. Inside were stacks of paper plates and cups. A tug on a drawer below yielded a view of plastic utensils.

"Only the best," she muttered under her breath, then braced herself for the contents of the refrigerator.

Surprisingly, there weren't any packages of decaying meat or moldy takeout. There was, in fact, almost nothing. A few bottles of soda, a bottle of beer, an apple and a small take-out container of coffee creamer.

"So like a man," she said aloud, returning to the living room. "Is this some new kind of diet?"

"I've been busy."

Her anger turned to pain. "Why?" she asked softly. "What did I do that was so horrible that you're not even comfortable coming to the Hip Hop for your meals? Do you think I'm going to punish you for not wanting to be friends anymore? Do you think I'm going to make a scene or talk about you behind your back?"

He lightly touched the bruise on his face. "It's not any of that, Darcy. I've been busy with work."

She glared at him. "Don't lie to me, Mark. I'm not stupid. This isn't about work. So what is it? What is going on between us? If you're tired of me, just say so. I can handle it."

He straightened. "It *is* about work and believe me, you don't want to know anything else."

"No! I want to know the truth. What's going on here?" She wanted to ask if this had something to do with their sexual encounters, but she didn't have the courage. She didn't want to know that Mark had changed his mind about wanting her in his bed.

He studied her for a long time. Pain filled his green eyes, but she had a bad feeling it wasn't about his twisted ankle.

"You're wrong about me," he said after a couple of minutes of silence. "This is completely work related. Our personal relationship complicates things for me.''

''What on earth could I have to do with your work?''

''We're involved, Darcy. I sure can't define our relationship, but we have one. The thing is I don't know if I can trust you. I know you're keeping secrets—you're hiding something about your past and you won't say why you moved to Whitehorn. There's a wad of cash in your living room and the sheriff has had an anonymous tip that someone is using the Hip Hop to launder money.''

Chapter Ten

Darcy stared at Mark for so long, he wondered if she'd heard him. Nothing about her expression changed. Then she turned and hurried toward the front door.

"Darcy?" he called.

She didn't bother looking back.

Mark leaned against the sofa and closed his eyes. No doubt he would get an award for jerk of the week, if there was such an honor. Could he have handled that worse than he did? He knew better than to simply blurt out that sort of information. Plus, something in his gut, something that had been there all along, told him she was innocent.

He should go after her, he thought, then realized he couldn't. Not only did his ankle ache, his crutches were on the far side of the room—well out of reach.

There was always crawling. Didn't women like that?

A cold draft blew across his cheek. He opened his eyes and saw that Darcy had left his front door open. The good news was, she was likely to return shortly. Or maybe not. Maybe her real plan was for him to freeze to death.

Apparently not, he thought less than two minutes later when she returned, slamming the door behind her. Fire blazed in her eyes as she thrust a bowl of leftover spaghetti at him. She fished the bottle of painkillers he'd been given at the hospital out of her jeans front pocket and tossed the container onto his lap. Then she disappeared into the kitchen only to return with a glass of water.

"This is so much more than you deserve," she told him, shaking with emotion. "I can't believe what you've thought of me."

"Darcy, you *do* have a secret life. You won't talk about your past in any reasonable way, then you disappeared for an entire day."

"So the obvious explanation is that I'm a criminal? Is that it? I don't spill my guts about every aspect of my life, so what? I launder money? Or maybe it's bigger than that. Have you thought of having my baked goods tested? Isn't it possible that I'm secretly distributing drugs to all my clients? How clever. Illegal substances in the pumpkin bread. I'm making gingerbread houses right now. Imagine what I could fill them with."

"Darcy—"

She planted her hands on her hips. "Shut up and

eat. You have to take a pill and you can't do that on an empty stomach."

"I'm sorry."

Her gaze narrowed. "Eat."

He took a bite of the spaghetti. Even a couple of days old, it was better than anything he'd had all week. He swallowed.

She nodded, as if satisfied he was going to follow instructions, then she headed for the door. "Don't forget your pills," she called over her shoulder and disappeared. The door slammed shut behind her.

Mark forced himself to eat a couple more forkfuls before popping a painkiller. Then he set the food on the coffee table and muttered several curses.

He'd blown it. There wasn't a doubt in his mind that he'd destroyed whatever fragile bond had been established between himself and Darcy. He'd acted like a jerk. He'd hurt her feelings and he didn't have anyone to blame but himself. All because of Sylvia.

He pictured his ex-fiancée. While Darcy was all soft curves and Midwest down-to-earth beauty, Sylvia had been slick, chic and very much in control. Looking back, he wondered what had affected him so. Had it been some kind of chemistry? Had he been so ready to fall for someone? Or had it been her supposed interest in him. She'd smiled as if she'd been waiting for him all her life, and had hung on every word. He hated to think he'd fallen for a great acting job, but he had a bad feeling that's what it all had been.

None of which was Darcy's fault. So why was he taking it out on her? Why was he making her pay for Sylvia's sins? He and Darcy weren't in love. They were friends who happened to be lovers. If anything he should be grateful. She'd reminded him that he was still alive and capable of sexual feeling. Being with her was better than being with anyone—even Sylvia. He'd—

The front door opened. Darcy stormed in, her arms holding a large brown paper bag. She kicked the door shut behind her and stalked to the coffee table where she shoved aside his half-eaten dinner.

Color stained her cheeks. Her curls were wild and there was still pain lurking in her eyes.

"I don't owe you this," she told him. "You've been stupid and insensitive from the start. If you had questions, you should have come to me with them. But no. You had to go your own macho way, assuming the worst. What did I ever do to you to make you think I'm a horrible person? I'm so angry, Mark. I trusted you with my friendship and with my body. You betrayed me."

"I'm sorry."

"Sorry doesn't cut it. Sorry is a weasel word. I wish there was a sword in here. I'd make you fall on it."

He was grateful she didn't mention his service revolver. "Darcy, if I don't tell you I'm sorry, what do you want me to say?"

"Nothing. I want you to listen."

She began emptying the paper bag. First she pulled out the music box, followed by a ledger and a folder. She handed him the music box.

"Count it," she said.

"Darcy…"

Her eyes turned to slits. "Count it."

He did as she requested. The bills were mostly fifties, with a few twenties and a one-hundred-dollar bill. "Three thousand one hundred and twenty dollars," he said.

She shoved the ledger at him. "If you remember, oh great detective, I have a side business. I sell baked goods."

A bad feeling swelled in the pit of his stomach. Damn. "But you're not up and running yet. You said you didn't have a contract with the Hip Hop."

"They're not the only place in town. I've catered several kids' parties, a volunteer luncheon and Ernie buys cookies from me to sell at his gas station." She leaned over the coffee table and flipped open the ledger. "This is my receivables list. An accounting of all the invoices I've issued and in this column is a list of the money I've received. Nearly everyone is paying me in cash, which I've noted here."

He followed the columns down to the bottom, where she'd totaled her invoices for the month of August. He turned to the next page and found listings for the next month, all the way through November.

She slapped the folder on top of the ledger. "These are my receipts for expenses. It just so happens that I total them for each month. If you subtract the expenses from the invoices, you'll find that in the past three months, my profits have been darned close to three thousand dollars."

The sinking feeling got worse. "Why didn't you put the money in the bank?"

"My paycheck gets automatically deposited. With

the baking, if I get paid in cash, I keep it cash and use the money for my expenses. And in case you want to accuse me of trying to avoid taxes, I can go get my quarterly returns.''

He closed the folder and the ledger, then handed both to her. Darcy knelt on the far side of the coffee table, looking at him as if he were something disgusting she'd found on the side of the road.

''I can't believe you thought I was laundering money,'' she told him. ''For one thing, if I was a criminal, don't you think I'd drive a better car? And why on earth would someone engage in that kind of criminal activity in Whitehorn? Everyone knows everyone else's business. It would be really hard to keep quiet. Plus, I've never been that stupid, or done anything illegal. And how could you make love with me all the while thinking I was a criminal?''

He leaned toward her, but she slid out of reach.

''I've only known about the money laundering for a couple of weeks.''

''Which is why you've been avoiding me.'' The pain in her eyes deepened. ''I didn't expect you to be the love of my life, Mark, but I did expect you to treat me like a friend. You couldn't even do that.''

He wanted to tell her that he hadn't thought she'd been the one laundering money, but he couldn't lie. She'd been the first person he'd thought of and he'd obsessed about the possibility ever since Rafe had come to see him. Why had he been so quick to judge her. And then he remembered. Sylvia.

Darcy pulled something else out of her bag. It was

a large photo album—old, worn and thick with pictures.

"About my secret life," she said slowly. "You're right. I have one. There's a really big thing I didn't tell you." She drew in a deep breath. "The thing is I didn't want to lose you. I knew that when you found out, you'd turn away and disappear just like every other guy has done. So I kept my secret."

Every muscle in his body stiffened. "You're married."

"What?" She stared at him as if he was crazy. "Married? I haven't even been on a date in five years. I'm not married."

Relief filled him. He figured he could handle about anything else. "Then what's the deep, dark secret?"

She shifted into a sitting position. "You interrupted my speech. I had some seriously righteous indignation going and now I forget where I was."

"You were saying that I would disappear when I found out the truth."

She paused, then nodded. "Well, now I want you gone so I'm going to tell you."

Her matter-of-fact words cut through him. While he hadn't expected his relationship with Darcy to lead anywhere, he didn't want it to end like this. "Okay. I'm a captive audience."

He reached for the photo album, but she put her hand on it to stop him. "You have to listen first. I told you that my parents died about five years ago, right?"

He nodded.

"I was telling the truth when I said they left me

almost nothing. By the time the bills were paid, I had a little money, but not much. What I didn't tell you is that I have a brother.''

Mark stared at her. "Why would you keep that a secret?"

"Because Dirk isn't like other kids. He's funny and handsome and I love him more than anyone in the world. He's also developmentally disabled. His problems put a big strain on my parents' marriage. I didn't get what the big deal was, but back then I rarely thought of anyone but myself. Dirk and I were buddies and I adored him. When my parents died, I knew I had to be responsible for both of us. Like I said, after the estate was settled, we didn't have much, but it was a small nest egg. Enough to get us through until I finished college and got a decent job.''

Obviously that hadn't happened, Mark thought, stunned by what Darcy had said. Questions filled his mind, but he held them in, wanting her to tell the story in her own way.

"Everything was going fine," she said, staring at the album rather than him. "Then one of Dirk's teachers decided I was too much of a flake to be responsible for someone with Dirk's special needs. He reported me to social services, they tried to take him away from me and we ended up in court. It took every penny left, but I managed to gain custody of my brother. That's when we left. I didn't want to stay in Chicago anymore.''

She rose to her feet, then paced to the window and stared out. Snow had started to fall. "I picked Arizona because there was a really good day school there for him. I managed to support us working two or three jobs. Dirk grew, but as he became a teenager things changed. He needed more.''

"The Madison School," Mark muttered. "That's why you moved here."

"Exactly. They have an amazing residential program. My brother is going to have wonderful opportunities to learn to function in the world. They expect him to be fairly self-sufficient in time. I just want him to be happy. One of the counselors there told me that we're in line for some financial aid, which is really good, because I'm hanging on by a thread. Every penny I make goes to my brother. I live as cheaply as I can. My car's old, my clothes are pathetic, I don't have a social life. And you know what? I don't give a damn, because I love my brother and I would do anything for him.''

She turned to face him. The rage had returned. "I work a fifty-hour week on my feet and I have a side business that just may turn out to be successful. So you have no right to judge me or accuse me of anything. I've done all this without one scrap of help and frankly I think I've done a hell of a job.''

She took a step toward him and planted her hands on her hips. "I thought you were pretty special. I actually liked you. Now I think you're scum and I'm sorry I ever slept with you. Go to hell, Mark Kincaid.''

She headed for the door and jerked it open. Then she aimed her parting shot. "By the way, I'm not pregnant. Not that you bothered to ask.''

She disappeared into the afternoon, slamming the door behind her.

Mark stared at the place where she'd stood and wished he could have a do-over. He'd blown this one from the beginning. The pain inside of him had nothing to do with his ankle or the bruise on his face. It came from having hurt someone who didn't deserve anything but the best that life had to offer.

When had he gotten so stupid?

Knowing it wasn't going to help but unable to stop himself, he reached for the album and put it on his lap. He turned the pages slowly and watched as Darcy's life unfolded before his eyes.

She'd been a chubby-cheeked little girl with blond curls and a perfect smile that made him ache. He saw pictures of her on a pony at a birthday party and in fancy dresses at the holidays. The background of the photos showed a large, elegant house with expensive furnishings. He saw her with friends, becoming school-age.

She was an awkward preadolescent when her brother arrived. There was a picture with her and a smiling baby. He flipped through photos of the two of them. Her parents' smiles became more strained, but Darcy's affection for Dirk was evident. He turned more pages and saw dance pictures, then prom photos. A beautiful Darcy with a handsome teenage boy. High school graduation followed, then pictures of just Dirk. He noticed there were far fewer of them than there had been of Darcy.

The last few pages showed a growing Dirk in a small apartment. The elegant furnishings were gone, as was the big house. Snapshots of Darcy showed her looking tired and thin. But the love between the siblings still shone out from every frame. He closed the book and set it back on the coffee table.

Darcy wasn't anything like Sylvia. He couldn't have been more wrong about her.

And now she was gone.

He tried to tell himself that this was better. He didn't want her in his life—he didn't want anyone. Her whole idea of being friends had been doomed from the start. He owed her an apology, of course, but after that it would be best if they simply returned to being neighbors who nodded when they saw each other. She wouldn't take too long to get over him. Being angry would help. As for him, he didn't have to recover—he'd never been involved.

It was odd, though, how the ache in his ankle was nothing when compared to the dull throbbing in his heart.

Darcy ignored the pieces of gingerbread still waiting to be assembled in her kitchen. She walked through the living room, down the short hall and entered her bedroom, where she threw herself on the bed. She hugged a pillow to her chest and waited for the tears burning at the back of her eyes to spill over.

Anger and confusion wrestled in her chest, and so far there was no clear winner. She was so mad at Mark that she could spit. She wanted to scream at him, demanding that he tell her where he got the right to judge her for something she hadn't even done. How dare he think she'd done something illegal? She hurt so much inside. He was gone from her life and somehow his leaving had left behind a really big hole.

She told herself she shouldn't care anymore. Mark had proved to be nothing more than a case of bad judgment. She wanted to justify what he'd thought of her by telling herself it was because he was a detective; thinking the worst of people was his job. But somehow she didn't buy into the explanation. He hadn't thought the worst of anyone else—just her.

She rolled onto her side, pulling the pillow with her. Despite how horrible she felt, there weren't any tears. They would probably come later, when she was ready to heal. But for now there was just the emptiness and the knowledge that she'd been foolish enough to allow herself to dream.

Darcy stood up. She tossed the pillow onto the bed and drew in a deep breath. If there was one thing the past five years had taught her, it was to keep moving forward, regardless of how daunting the circumstances. She had orders to fill and a life to live. If Mark Kincaid wanted to be an ass, that was his business, not hers.

Four hours later she'd finished assembling the two gingerbread houses. The three she'd already completed had been loaded into boxes that she'd carefully carried to her car, along with seven dozen cookies. She began her deliveries around four, grateful that the snow had stopped.

Promptly at five she pulled into the parking lot of the Hip Hop Café. Melissa North, the owner of the café, was back from her vacation and had wanted to sample Darcy's goods for the following week.

Darcy grabbed the cookies first, and headed for the front of the café. She knocked on the closed and locked door.

From where she stood she could see two people inside. Melissa stood talking to a man. Darcy squinted, then recognized Josh Anderson. They walked to the front door and Melissa turned the key in the lock.

"You're right on time," Melissa said. The store owner was of medium height, with beautiful black hair and intense blue eyes. She smiled, then sniffed. "Something smells heavenly."

"Cookies," Darcy admitted. "I have the gingerbread house in the car."

"I'll go get it," Josh said.

"Thanks."

Darcy moved aside to let him out. Melissa returned her attention to the diner. "Josh and I were discussing remodeling the café. I have this idea about making it a little more upscale. Maybe get in a dinner crowd rather than just the burger set."

"Upscale means higher prices," Darcy said with a laugh. "My tips go up with the prices, so I'm in favor of expansion."

Melissa grinned. "I'll put you down in the yes column, then."

"What about a health food menu to supplement the regular entrées?"

Josh returned with the box. "I heard that," he said. "Don't let her talk you into it, Melissa. Montana isn't tofu country."

He walked over to the long counter and set the box

down by the cash register. Darcy knew he was just teasing. There was no way he could know that the mention of tofu made her think of Mark, which made her shoulders slump.

"There are other healthy choices," Darcy insisted. "Maybe something meatless."

Melissa smiled. "I'll think about it. In the meantime, I'd love to see what you've brought."

Darcy set her box of cookies on a table, then opened the box containing the house. She unfastened the sides, peeling them back to expose her Christmas treat. Candies decorated the sides and roof of the house. Icing "snow" edged the windows. She'd used chocolate cookie fingers to make a fence and chocolate-covered graham crackers for a pathway.

Melissa clapped her hands together. "It's fabulous. Did you really make it yourself?"

Her obvious pleasure eased some of Darcy's hollowness. She nodded. "Once the main structure is together, it's not that difficult to do. Just lots of candy, icing and patience."

Josh reached for a gumdrop. Darcy pushed his arm away. "Don't make me hurt you. If you want something to eat, try a cookie."

"What's in them?" he asked suspiciously.

"Plenty of butter and sugar. It's the holidays and I try not to think about calories in December."

Still looking doubtful, Josh opened the second box and pulled out an iced cookie. He took a bite, then nodded. "This works," he mumbled.

Melissa reached for one, as well. After she tasted the cookie, she sighed. "It's delicious enough to cause me to make noises that shouldn't be heard outside of the bedroom. Janie was right. Your baked goods are terrific. Let's talk tomorrow after your shift. If you're still interested, we can work out a deal to have you supply the café.''

"I'd like that," Darcy said, hoping she sounded excited.

She should be happy. She *was* happy. She'd worked hard for this opportunity. If she got a baking contract with the Hip Hop Café, she wouldn't have to sweat her monthly bills—especially for Dirk's school—so much. And if he received some financial aid, she might be able to draw a breath and actually slow down.

"Then I'll see you here tomorrow," Melissa said, pulling a datebook out of her oversize purse. "I'd like you to bring me a list of what baked goods you'll provide, and a schedule. We'll have to play with quantities for a while until we figure out how much we can sell."

"Not a problem."

Darcy already had all that information in a notebook at home. She would make a copy during her break tomorrow and have it ready for Melissa by the time of their meeting.

She excused herself so Josh and Melissa could finish their conversation on remodeling, and made her way to her car.

She was excited, she told herself. Darned excited. This was a great opportunity. Yes, there would be extra work, but she'd held as many as three jobs at a time before, so she was used to long hours and little sleep. If nothing else, keeping busy would help her get over Mark quicker. She wasn't going to have much time to think about him.

She started her car, then waited for the engine to warm up. The thing was, she thought, resting her forehead on the steering wheel, she couldn't start getting over him until the horrible empty feeling inside of her went away. She couldn't remember ever being so sad about the loss of a relationship. Which didn't make sense. After her parents died and all her friends had faded away, she'd felt completely abandoned. But somehow this was different. Worse.

Something about knowing Mark was forever out of her life made it very difficult to even breathe.

Mark sat alone in his living room and watched the light fade as afternoon turned to evening. He told himself he should get some ice for his ankle and maybe take another pain pill. He should do a lot of things. But instead of getting up, he simply closed his eyes and wished he could turn back the clock.

Why had he thought Darcy was the one involved with the money laundering? Now, with hindsight, he could see that he'd been completely wrong about her. There was nothing in her background or her life that even hinted at anything illegal. Yet he'd thought of her first. Finding the money had only confirmed his suspicions.

Because he'd wanted it to be her.

The thought struck him like a sucker punch. He lightly touched the throbbing bump on his face, then shook his head. Damn. Why hadn't he seen it before?

He'd wanted Darcy to be the bad guy because then he could dismiss her from his life. He wouldn't have to worry about liking her or not liking her. He wouldn't have to reconcile what he'd been through with Sylvia with his present situation. He could stay comfortably angry with the world for being such a rotten place and with himself for being so stupid and blind.

The memory of the hurt and shock in her eyes made him squirm. He'd done her wrong in the most fundamental way possible. He'd damaged her character.

She was a woman who had given up everything she'd ever known to take care of her brother. With no experience, she'd survived in a hostile world. Then he'd come along and had accused her of being a criminal because that was a whole lot easier than thinking she might be a pretty terrific person that he was in danger of falling for.

He wanted to take his accusations back. He wanted a second chance. Not because he had any expectations, but because someone like Darcy didn't show up in a guy's life very often. She'd wanted to be his friend. He'd never considered that much of an honor, but he'd been wrong.

He swore under his breath. He couldn't make it right, but he could explain. He owed her that. He knew she would still walk away—she might be soft-hearted, but she wasn't stupid. She wouldn't trust him with a second chance.

After dropping off the rest of her baked goods, Darcy pulled in front of her apartment. Something large and dark sat on her front steps. As her headlights swept across the duplex, she saw the large, dark something move. Mark?

She set the parking brake, then turned off the engine. No. He couldn't be here. It was cold and the snow was due to start up any second.

"Are you crazy?" she asked as she climbed out of her car. "What are you doing? You're supposed to be keeping your leg elevated."

"Would you believe I ran out of ice? I thought maybe if I stuck my foot in snow it would do the same thing."

She pulled her coat closer around her body. The cold burned her skin and her eyes. As she approached the porch, she saw Mark was huddled on the top step. He had his bad foot buried in snow. She didn't want to think about how much it would have hurt him to pull on a boot, even though he hadn't fastened it. She refused to feel sorry for him.

"Why are you here?" she asked, stopping in front of him.

Instead of answering, he held out several thin boxes. "A peace offering," he said. "Christmas lights. I can't put them up right now, but maybe by midweek." He hesitated. "I know you're a sucker for Christmas."

"Apparently I'm a sucker for a lot of things."

He nodded. "At the risk of you leaving me out here in the snow to freeze to death, I'm going to ask you to invite me in."

His boldness stunned her. "Why would I do that?

So you can say more terrible things about me? What do you want to accuse me of now? Has there been a murder in town? Am I the prime suspect?''

He gazed at her. ''I want to apologize and explain.''

''No explanation is necessary. Besides, you couldn't possibly come up with a story good enough.''

Something flickered in his eyes. Something dark and painful. Something that made her heartache ease slightly and her resolve waver.

''Actually, I could,'' he told her. ''Let me try, Darcy. I know what I did was awful. I'm really sorry. You didn't deserve my accusations, but they're made and now I would like to explain them.''

She didn't want to hear what he had to say. Yet she couldn't bring herself to deny him.

''Once a sucker, always a sucker,'' she muttered as she bent low to help him to his feet. ''This had better be good.''

Chapter Eleven

Darcy helped Mark to her sofa, then eased him out of his coat. She ignored the feel of his body so close to hers. No way was she still attracted to the man.

She also ignored the three boxes of outdoor lights he'd brought her, along with the fact that he couldn't have just gone out and bought them today. Which meant he'd had them for some time. As she doubted that he'd planned on putting them up at his place—the man didn't even own dishes, let alone Christmas decorations—he must have bought them for her. Which meant he'd been thinking of her in a positive way. Which did *not* begin to make up for all he'd accused her of today.

"How's your ankle?" she asked grudgingly as she took off her coat.

"Sore," he admitted.

She hung up both their coats, then returned to the sofa. After sitting on the coffee table, she reached for his boot and eased it off his injured foot. She could feel the heat from the swelling.

"You shouldn't have come over," she told him. "You didn't even use your crutches."

"I thought they might slip in the snow."

The man was impossible. "You could have phoned in your explanation."

"You would have hung up on me."

That much was true, she thought, almost wishing he wasn't here now. Part of her didn't want to hear his explanation. For one thing, she doubted it would be enough to convince her that he was anything but the bad guy in this. For another, she didn't want to give him a chance to trick her into starting to like him again.

She eased his sock-clad foot onto a small throw pillow. "Don't think I'm going to let you off the hook easily," she told him. "I'm angry and hurt and I have no intention of forgiving you."

"I know. That's not why I'm here. I want you to know why it happened, but I don't expect anything else to change."

She glared at him, but he didn't try to justify his position more. She rose. "I hate that I feel compelled to offer you something to eat. Did you finish the spaghetti?"

"Most of it."

She sighed, then headed for the kitchen. After the loss of her parents, she'd been surprised to find out that she was something of a caretaker. She enjoyed giving to people. If money and space weren't an issue, not to mention her long workdays, she would fill her place with homeless dogs and cats. Even now, when she should want to rip out Mark's heart, she couldn't help fixing hot chocolate and piling cookies on a plate.

She returned to the living room and set the tray on the sofa next to him, then grabbed a mug for herself and retreated to a chair across the room.

"Start talking," she said, hoping she sounded furious. Unfortunately, her rage and indignation seemed to have faded some, leaving her feeling only empty and sad.

Twenty-four hours ago, she would have been dying to tell him about her new contract at the Hip Hop. Of course, then he hadn't known about Dirk, so he wouldn't have understood why it was so important for her to earn money. Now he knew about Dirk, but they weren't friends anymore.

Her chest tightened at the thought. Not friends. Funny how in just a few weeks Mark had become an important part of her life. Initially she'd had a crush on him but, as she'd gotten to know him, she'd found herself liking him for the man he was, not just who she imagined him to be.

"I'm sorry," he said quietly. "For thinking badly of you. When I knew you had a secret in your life, I assumed the worst."

She glared at him over her mug. "You could have asked."

"Agreed." He took a sip of the hot chocolate.

"Thank you for telling me about your brother. I wish it had happened under other circumstances."

She shifted her gaze to stare at the wall behind him. "I stopped telling people a long time ago. I got tired of being disappointed by people I liked."

"I don't think I would have disappointed you about that."

She wanted to believe that was true but had her doubts. "Maybe not, but you disappointed me about other things."

"I know. Looking back, I don't understand how I could have thought those things about you. You're a good person, one of the best people I know."

She returned her attention to him, trying not to notice how green his eyes looked in the lamplight or how the shape of his mouth made her remember how good it had been between them.

"You're stalling," she said. "Do you actually have something to tell me, or was this all a smoke screen?"

He drew in a deep breath. "You're right. I don't want to tell you this, because it's going to change the way you think about me."

"It's not going to get worse than how it is now."

"I hope you're right."

For the first time since inviting him inside, Darcy felt a shiver of apprehension. While she didn't doubt Mark thought he had a great reason for thinking so badly of her, she didn't expect to be impressed. But now, looking at the haunted expression in his eyes, she began to wonder.

"After college I left here for New York," he said. "I was accepted into the New York police department. My goal had always been to make detective. When I was sixteen and still in high school, I worked part-time for old Scott Riley who ran a sleazy little detective agency here in town. The work was mostly finding out if a spouse was having an affair, but occasionally there was a great case.''

''And this is interesting how?'' Darcy asked with more temper than she felt. She didn't want to get sucked into Mark's past. What did it have to do with her?

''I'm getting to the point,'' he said. ''But it's going to take me a minute.''

She rose and crossed to the sofa, where she grabbed two cookies before returning to her chair. She nibbled on the first one. Maybe the sugar would take the edge off, she thought.

''My career skyrocketed right away,'' he continued. ''I worked long hours, but I loved it. I got involved in a couple of high-profile crimes and worked with some great detectives. I learned a lot and when the time came, they put in a good word for me. So there I was, in New York, living my dream. The only down side was my personal life.''

Darcy forced herself to swallow her mouthful of cookies, but she suddenly felt sick inside. ''I don't think I want to hear this.''

''Sorry, but it's the only story I know.'' He shifted on the sofa. ''I dated a lot, but I never felt anything. I mean I liked some of them fine, but there wasn't any spark.''

Darcy suddenly found it difficult to look at the sofa where she and Mark had about set each other on fire.

"I wanted to get married," he said. "I wanted kids, a family, but it wasn't happening. By the time I'd been a detective for two years, I was starting to have second thoughts about my career choice. I saw a side to people I didn't like. Once I got transferred to homicide, I figured there wasn't any humanity left in the world. I know it sounds stupid, but I thought I could feel my soul drying up. One day it was going to shrivel up and blow away. And then I met Sylvia."

Darcy froze. She shouldn't have been surprised, she told herself. She'd known from the minute Mark had mentioned the woman's death that she'd been important to him. She put down the remaining cookie and her hot chocolate. Her stomach felt queasy.

"We lived next door to each other," he said, not looking at her, as he proceeded to tell her about meeting the woman he'd wanted to marry.

Darcy listened, though every word was torture. Her face burned and her mouth went dry. She'd been right before—she didn't want to hear this story. But she also couldn't bring herself to stop him. Maybe it was like driving by an accident. She didn't want to look but she couldn't help herself.

"Did you marry her?" she asked without thinking. Had Mark been married before? She'd never considered that a possibility.

"No. I never even proposed, although I did buy a ring. I never gave it to her."

"Why?" She spoke past the pain, which wasn't very easy.

He shrugged. "I wanted to get to know her better. I wanted to be sure. Intellectually I knew I was running on hormones.'' He took a drink of his hot chocolate. ''About two months into the relationship, I got a frantic call from her. I was at work. It was late. I think I was doing paperwork, I don't remember. She sounded hysterical as she begged me to come home. When I got there, I found a dead man in her kitchen.''

Darcy blinked. She'd braced herself for several different possibilities, but that wasn't one of them. ''Someone had tried to kill her?''

''No. It took me a while to get any information out of her. At first she said the guy was an intruder, but it turns out he was her husband.''

Darcy couldn't believe it. ''She was married?''

He nodded. ''It took me by surprise, too. She said that she'd been separated for a long time and that she'd wanted to tell me but was afraid it would change things between us. I was too shocked to know what to think. She said they hadn't spoken in weeks. She'd been out shopping and had returned to find him dead in her kitchen. She didn't know what to do.''

''I can't blame her.'' Darcy knew a dead body in her house would leave her pretty hysterical, too.

''I should have known,'' he continued quietly. ''The fact that she hadn't told me about being married was a big red flag, but I thought I loved her so I ignored it.''

Darcy tried not to mind that Mark had been so willing to believe the best of Sylvia but think the worst of her.

''I called the precinct,'' he said. ''I knew the guys working the murder. I couldn't get involved because I knew Sylvia, but I was kept advised of what was going on. At first they weren't sure, but then one day the detectives on the case brought me in for a private conversation. It seems that the evidence pointed to the fact that Sylvia had killed her husband herself.''

On the one hand, Darcy wasn't surprised by the revelation. On the other hand, she couldn't believe it. "Why?"

"I don't know. She never said."

"You talked to her about it?"

"Oh, yeah. I went to her place and confronted her with the facts. At first she tried to deny everything. She cried and said that she loved me. If I loved her, too, I would believe her."

"But you didn't?"

"I was starting to have my doubts. Finally she admitted she'd done it and she expected me to help her get away with it. When I refused, she threatened me. When I still wouldn't go along with her plan, she pulled a gun and shot me. Twice.''

Darcy nearly fainted. She felt all the blood rush from her head to her feet and the room began to sway. She gasped for breath. Gradually the room stilled and she was able to see Mark. He sat across from her, watching her. Probably trying to judge her reaction.

"She's the reason you were injured? I thought some criminal did it."

"She was a murderer."

She brushed aside his comment with a flick of her wrist. "You know what I mean. I thought it had happened during a chase or something."

"I guess we all have our secrets."

He was acting flip, but she doubted he felt as calm

on the inside. Questions filled her mind, even as puzzle pieces clicked into place. No wonder he'd assumed the worst about her.

"What happened after she shot you?"

"She was arrested for the murder of her husband and for attempting to kill me. I spent a lot of time in the hospital and then in rehabilitation."

She thought about the still-healing scars on his body. "You could have died."

"That's what the doctors said."

"You must have been in shock for a long time," she said more to herself than to him. "You'd been planning to marry this woman."

"The irony of the situation doesn't escape me," he admitted. "While I was recovering, I had plenty of time to think. What I still can't get over is how wrong I was about her. I was a cop—a detective. I'm supposed to know people, but she fooled me completely. So much for being a good judge of character."

She was torn between wanting to point out that he'd blown it about her, too, and the need to walk over to the sofa, sit next to him and pull him close. Instead she stayed where she was.

"I keep asking myself how she could have tricked me," he admitted. "At the same time I was recovering from being shot and mentally ending the relationship. Knowing how she'd used me violated everything I thought I knew about myself, her... everyone. It changed my view of the world. I used to think that whole stages of mourning was a lot of crap, but I went through them all. Although I think I stalled in anger for a while."

"That's understandable. What happened to Sylvia after the arrest?"

He shrugged. "She entered a plea. They refused bail. The charges against her included lying in wait, which judges frown upon. So she changed her plea. It was a mess. There was a bunch of media attention. When I was well enough, I left it all behind and moved back here."

She tried to absorb what he'd told her. "If she'd lived, would you have had to go back to New York to testify?"

"Yeah, and I wasn't looking forward to it. Once I got back to Whitehorn, I just wanted to stay put." He stared at her. "The point of this isn't to make you feel sorry for me, but to help you understand why I have a problem trusting women."

"I do. In a way." She sighed. "The thing is, I'm not Sylvia."

"I know. I should have seen that right away. But there were too many similarities. You lived next door. You're attractive, we got along well."

Sex. He was talking about sex. "You do seem to have a thing for spontaneous combustion," she said with a lightness she didn't feel.

"Actually that's a new experience for me," he said. "I've never had what we've had."

Darcy didn't dare analyze the relief she felt at his words. She also had a couple of questions. How would he define what they had? What were they to each other?

His story had done what he'd claimed—she was no longer so angry with him and she could almost forgive him for what he'd done. But she hated that all of this had been because of another woman. A woman he'd wanted to marry. Have children with. Someone he'd wanted for more than just sex.

"No wonder you were devastated when she killed herself," Darcy said.

"I was surprised," he told her. "Not devastated."

"I'm not sure I believe you."

"You don't have to. I'm working on closure. Sometimes I think I should forgive her, or maybe just myself. At times I can almost feel sorry for her. When I look back on our relationship, what I think about is how stupid I'd been and how could I have let that happen." He shifted slightly, then grimaced as his ankle turned. "I have a lot of questions and no answers. The one thing I do know is that I never loved her."

"If you wanted to marry her, then you did a good job of faking it."

"I think it was more of a matter of being in the right place at the right time. I had the career I'd always wanted, things were going well. Looking back, I wonder if I was so enamored with her because I was ready to have a family. I wanted to get married and she was there."

Darcy wished it was that simple, but she knew the truth was far more complex. "You said you'd been out with a lot of different women and none of them clicked with you. Obviously there was something special about Sylvia."

He looked at her. "The woman killed her husband in cold blood and then expected me to help her cover up the crime. I don't think 'special' quite describes it."

"You know what I mean. You had strong feelings for her."

He nodded absently, as if he was thinking about something else. Darcy tried to search her own heart to figure out what was going on inside. Once again Mark had confused her to the point of practically gasping for air. Every time she thought she had him figured out, he stumped her.

Despite what he'd done to her, she couldn't hate him. Worse, she felt herself softening toward him, as if she were about to start liking him again. What was that old saying? *Fool me once, shame on you, fool me twice, shame on me.* Was she about to be a fool for this man again?

Mark moved a little, so there was more room next to him on the sofa. He patted the seat cushion. She folded her arms over her chest but otherwise didn't move.

"We can talk fine with me sitting over here," she said primly, not daring to move closer. Her heart might not know what was going on, but that didn't mean her body wasn't ready to go up in flames at the slightest provocation.

"I agree that we can have a conversation, but I won't know that we're okay," he said. "I want to know that we can still be friends."

Friends. It was what she'd wanted, so why did his declaration disappoint her?

"We're friends."

"You still look pissed off."

"I'm not."

"You're all scrunchy. Your arms are crossed and your eyes look all disapproving. You're not even smiling. So you still hate me."

"I don't hate you."

"There must be a reason you're still crabby."

She sucked in a breath. "I'm *not* crabby," she said, her voice practically a growl.

"You really sound crabby," he murmured, then picked up a cookie and took a bite.

She raised her arms, palms up. "What do you want from me?"

"Nothing. I'm fine."

He sounded hurt. She ignored his heavy sigh and the dispirited way he ate the cookie. She would not be sucked into feeling guilty when all of this was his fault.

"Do you think you'll ever forgive me?" he asked.

"I forgive you now."

"You're just saying that."

Her patience snapped. "Fine. You win."

She rose and stalked over to the sofa, then plopped down next to him. "There. Are you happy?"

He grinned. "Yes."

"Figures. You are so annoying. You make me want to kick you in the ankle."

He winced. "That would be mean. Where did this mean streak come from?"

Darcy leaned back against the sofa and closed her eyes. "I only have myself to blame," she muttered under her breath. "I could have left him outside to freeze, but no. I had to be all neighborly and caring. I had to let him inside.''

''Darcy?''

''What?'' she snapped without looking at him.

''I'm really sorry. I treated you badly. My past with Sylvia explains my actions, but it doesn't excuse them. If I had suspicions, I should have come to you right away. I went behind your back and I punished you for things you hadn't done. That was wrong.''

His heartfelt apology accomplished what all the teasing hadn't. She melted inside. ''It's okay,'' she said.

''No, it's not. But I hope we can recover from this.''

She nodded. ''We can.''

He offered her a cookie. She took one, but before she could bite into it, he spoke again.

''Thanks for telling me about not being pregnant.''

Darcy carefully put the cookie back on the plate. ''Yes, well, I would have told you before, but you weren't around. I found out last week.''

''Are you okay with that?''

''Not being pregnant? Of course. Why would you ask?'' A baby? Now? A baby was about the last thing she needed in her life.

''I wanted to be sure. Sometimes a close call gets people thinking.''

''Are you speaking from personal experience?''

''No, but it happened to my partner when I was in New York. His wife thought she was pregnant. They already had a couple of kids, and weren't sure they wanted more. They agonized over it, then when they'd finally decided they were thrilled with the idea of another child, she found out she wasn't pregnant. They were both devastated.''

"Not my situation at all," she assured him.

"Just checking."

She started to ask him if he was okay when she felt a slight clenching around her heart. A faint stab of…what? Longing, she thought. Longing for a child of her own.

She'd never really allowed herself to dream about something like that. After all, she had plenty of responsibilities and no one to share them with. A child would make her situation impossible. And yet, now that Mark had asked the question, she couldn't help wondering what it would be like to have a baby with him.

Instantly she pictured a pretty green-eyed, dark-haired little girl holding hands with her blond, blue-eyed brother. She and Mark would have made amazing babies together, she thought sadly.

She jerked herself out of her daydream with a stern warning not to go there. Wanting a baby with a man was a slick road to disaster. Next up she'd be thinking about a permanent relationship. Or falling in love.

"Darcy? Are you all right?"

"I'm fine."

Love? No. Not in this lifetime. Not with any man and especially not with Mark.

"What were you thinking?" he asked.

She avoided his gaze. "Just that I'm glad we've been responsible since that first time. You've been really good about wearing a condom."

"I'm happy to do it."

If sex was going to be a part of her life, she needed to take precautions. This time she'd gotten off lightly, but what if she had been pregnant? The odds of her getting involved with anyone seemed slim, but it obviously *could* happen.

"Maybe I should go on the Pill," she said, more to herself than him.

"An interesting idea."

Heat flared in her cheeks as she realized what she'd just said aloud. "Oh! I didn't mean to say that. I, ah, just..." She drew in a breath. "I was thinking out loud. I wasn't hinting."

He lightly touched her arm. "I've missed you."

She knew what he meant. He'd missed her *in bed.* She wanted to say she hadn't missed him. That she didn't want a physical relationship with him. Not anymore. Unfortunately she'd never been much of a liar.

She breathed his name.

For a man with a swollen ankle, he moved darned fast, she thought as he eased closer and wrapped an arm around her.

She told herself to resist. She told herself to pull away. Sex with Mark always made her life more complicated. They'd barely gotten one mess straightened out—did she really want to make a new one?

He lightly kissed her mouth. Her resolve faded like so much mist as her body went on alert.

"I don't want to start trouble," she said, even as she wiggled closer to him.

"We make the best kind of trouble," he whispered, and deepened the kiss.

Chapter Twelve

Darcy thought about trying to convince herself that she was being swept away against her will when the truth was she wanted to be with Mark. Being close to him might weaken her resolve to the point where she didn't have a whole lot of choice in the matter, but that was her problem. Not his. She and Mark created some kind of sensual magic when they were together.

He cupped her face, his fingers warm and gentle as they rested on her cheek. His mouth moved against hers, his tongue stroking her lower lip. His scent surrounded her. Although they'd only made love a handful of times, the moment felt familiar. She knew how he would taste when she parted for him. She anticipated the lean strength of his body, the way his arousal would press against her. She knew his touch, his heat, his need.

Such knowledge implied an intimacy that frightened her. Her first instinct was to push him away. But her longing was too intense. She could only part her lips and surrender, hoping she was smart enough to keep her heart out of reach.

His tongue brushed against hers. She moaned softly as feeling swept through her. Her breasts grew more sensitive as her nipples tightened, pushing against her bra. Between her legs, familiar need made her insides heavy as her body anticipated their joining.

As she went to wrap her arms around him, she found herself trapped against the sofa. Sitting next to each other made the logistics awkward at best. She started to move, then remembered his tender ankle.

"We have a problem," she said, pulling away and gazing at him.

He took her hand and drew it down to his crotch. "I think maybe 'massive' would be a better description. Certainly not 'problem.'"

She closed her fingers around his arousal. Just knowing how much he wanted her made her go all soft. Soft to his hard. She shivered slightly.

"I meant your ankle," she said. "Our positions here are a little awkward. I'm not sure how to make it easier."

"You could help me into your bedroom."

"Yes, I could."

She rose to her feet, then helped him to his. An hour ago, she'd been furious and hurt. Now she simply wanted to make love with him.

They moved slowly toward the hall. He hopped, while allowing her to support some of his weight. When they entered her bedroom, they headed for the bed. Mark sat on the mattress, then reached for her, pulling her between his parted legs.

"What about your ankle?" she asked as she wrapped her arms around his shoulders and bent toward him.

"Let me worry about that."

They kissed, tongues circling and dancing in a pattern they'd created for just the two of them. The deep, intimate contact made her toes curl. His hands leisurely stroked up and down her back, drawing her closer while touching her all over. He cupped her rear, squeezing the curves, then stroked her hips. From there his hands journeyed up toward her chest.

He avoided her breasts, instead running his fingers along her arms. Even through her long-sleeved shirt she felt the warmth of his touch. She shivered, then sighed.

He returned to her waist where he pulled her shirt free of her jeans. As he nibbled her lower lip and breathed her name, he began to unfasten the buttons. One by one. Slowly. Cool air tickled along her bare skin, then her shoulders and arms as he drew off the shirt. He reached for her bra hooks and unfastened them. She dropped her arms to her side and let the garment slip to the floor.

Her breasts were already swollen in anticipation, her nipples tight. When he broke the kiss on her lips, she caught her breath in anticipation of those same actions repeated on another sensitive spot.

He read her mind. His hands pressed on her back, urging her forward until he licked her right nipple. Darcy held in a scream. Fire flared from that single point of contact, heating her other breast, her chest, then searing down between her legs. She felt herself dampen instantly. Her jeans felt too tight. Hunger filled her—hunger brought on by a need so powerful she knew she would die if he didn't touch her intimately.

He licked her, moving from breast to breast, then breathing against the valley between. He bent his head and nipped the sensitive skin on her side.

"I want you," he said, raising his gaze to hers.

She saw the need in his eyes, the passion flaring there. She bent to kiss him, as she reached for the buttons on his shirt.

Her fingers fumbled as her tongue mated with his. Laughing softly, they broke apart to remove the rest of their clothes.

"We need to be careful," she reminded him as he gingerly removed the sock on his swollen ankle. "Are you sure about this?"

Mark pulled off his briefs. His arousal sprang free. "Does that answer your question?"

Her gaze lingered on that most male part of him. She liked the shape of him, the way she could hold him and feel the heavy pulse of his blood.

"It's a very visual reply," she murmured.

He eased himself back on the bed. "I don't think we're going to have a problem," he said. "As long as you don't mind being on top."

Darcy had never been completely comfortable with her body. At least not in the company of other people. But with Mark she felt safe. He'd touched every part of her and his obvious pleasure in pleasing her had made her stop worrying that she wasn't perfect enough.

"I can be on top," she told him, then imagined herself straddling him, his arousal thrusting into her.

"Good, then come here."

He drew her to him, shifting her so that they faced each other. She stared into his eyes, watching his pupils dilate when she reached down to stoke him.

"Two can play at that game," he teased, brushing her hand away and slipping his fingers between her thighs.

He found her point of pleasure instantly. She was already swollen and oh, so ready. Her eyes closed of their own accord as she lost herself in the feeling of him touching her. He'd already learned the rhythm she preferred. Slow, then faster as she got closer.

Over and over, the steady stroking brought her to the edge of madness. He stopped to shift her legs, then continued. But this time was different. She felt his hardness probing. Instinctively she arched toward him, trying to draw him in. But because of their positions he could only enter a little bit, then he retreated. Her inner muscles clenched tightly, as if they could will him to be inside of her. Anticipation fueled her desire. She found herself moving closer and closer as her body tensed.

"Tell me just before," he whispered.

She forced herself to open her eyes. "Why?"

"I'm gonna stop."

"Mark!"

"You'll like it. I promise."

Her eyelids sank closed as he began to move faster. Tension spiraled nearly out of control. She didn't want to stop. She wanted this to go on forever. She wanted—

"Now!" she cried.

As promised, he removed his fingers. She gasped in disappointment as the intensity subsided slightly. Then she noticed that he was still pushing against her. Going in a tiny bit, but not fully. All her attention focused on that place where they touched. Tension began to grow again.

He teased her with his not-quite-entering until she was breathless and begging. Then he stopped that, too.

Darcy knew she was going to die. Or explode. She couldn't stand it. Not like this. She had to—they had to—

Still on his side, he bent down and licked her nipple. The contact was better than it had been before. Every part of her was sensitized. She rolled onto her back, offering herself to him. He bent over her, sucking deeply, using his fingers on one nipple, his tongue on the other. He touched and tormented until a sheen of perspiration covered her body. She could barely catch her breath.

Finally he raised his head. "About that protection we were discussing earlier."

She reached for the box of condoms in her night-stand. Her fingers shook as she slipped one on him.

"I'd like you to get on top of me," he whispered, then smiled a smile that promised paradise. "Slowly."

She did as he requested, first rising to her knees, then straddling him. He was hard and ready, slipping easily into her waiting wetness. She was so ready. So close. Her first instinct was to ride him. He grabbed her hips to hold her still.

"Slow," he repeated.

Her breath caught. She couldn't go slow. She would die. Or explode. Or both.

It was agony, but she forced herself to raise up in millimeters, then settle back on his length. With her second stroke, he reached between their bodies and rubbed her swollen center.

The unexpected caress was more than she could stand. She found herself shattering without warning. All thoughts of slow went out of her mind as she pulsed her hips and lost herself in the sensations shooting through her. He continued to rub her, then suddenly he clutched her hips and groaned. She felt him stiffen.

The last of her contractions faded as contentment filled her. When he drew her into his arms, she went willing, resting her head on his chest and listening to the rapid thunder of his heart.

They snuggled under the covers. Darcy breathed in Mark's scent and sighed with happiness. Maybe she was being foolish, allowing herself to connect physically with this man, but she couldn't find it in her heart to feel regret. Maybe that would come later, but for now there was only a sense of belonging.

Mark wrapped his arms around her and stroked her hair, wrapping her curls around his fingers, then releasing them.

"I've missed you," he told her. "I missed talking to you."

She didn't want to analyze his words too much, or read more into them than he meant, so she settled for the easiest, most honest response.

"Me, too."

"Tell me what's been going on in your life since we were last together."

"I got the baking contract at the Hip Hop. I'm going to see Melissa tomorrow after my shift and we'll decide on what I'll be baking and how much."

"Hey, that's great." He squeezed her. "Are you going to have to give up sleep to get it all done?"

"Maybe. But it's worth it." She hesitated. "I'm not trying to get rich. I need the money to pay for Dirk's school."

Mark rolled onto his back and settled her with her head on his shoulder. "I've never been to the Madison School, but I've heard about it. It has a great reputation."

"I know." She tilted her head so she could look at him. "We knew pretty early that there was something different about Dirk. My dad completely freaked out. He wouldn't have anything to do with him. My mom went in the other direction. She became completely absorbed with his problems, and wanted to fix him. When she found out there wasn't a cure for what he had, she turned her back on him, as well.''

Darcy pressed her hand against Mark's chest. ''I was too into my own life to realize what was going on. To me, Dirk was my brother. I loved him, we had fun together. End of story. It wasn't until my parents died and I was responsible for him that I began to worry about his future.''

''Is he the reason you moved to Arizona?''

''Part of it. There was a decent school where we were, but after all our friends abandoned us, I didn't see the point in staying. I wanted to try living somewhere warm. Dirk was in a day program there and he was really doing well, but as he got older, he needed more.''

''How old is he?''

''Fourteen.'' She smiled. ''He's a great kid. Funny and caring. But he's growing taller every year and it became difficult to find a baby-sitter for when I wasn't home. Plus he needed more one-on-one attention. I found out about the Madison School. They're different in that they focus on preparing teenagers like Dirk for the real world. They have a fabulous staff and an excellent curriculum.''

''How do you pay for it?''

She raised herself up on her elbow. ''Not by laundering money.''

''Ouch.''

She lightly kissed him. ''Sorry. I was teasing. Actually I've been getting by. I had some savings when we moved here and the school lets me pay monthly.

That money you saw in my music box is my entire savings account.''

''You shouldn't keep it in cash.''

''I know. But I get paid in cash and getting to the bank is one more thing I don't have time to do. The good news is that one of Dirk's counselors told me that he thinks we'll be eligible for financial aid. I'm trying not to get my hopes up, but if they could cover even half of his school, it would be a huge help.''

''And in the meantime you work two jobs.''

She shrugged. ''I've worked three before. This is hardly new to me.''

He studied her, his green eyes dark and unreadable. ''You're an amazing woman, Darcy Montague. I'm impressed.''

His words made her feel all warm inside. ''Don't be. I'm just taking care of my brother. It's not all that different from what you did with your sister when your parents died.''

''It's very different. I looked after Maddie for a couple of years. You've signed up for a lifetime of commitment.''

His words made her uncomfortable. Not because of the praise, but because she suspected she knew what was coming next. Now that Mark knew about her brother and all that was involved with caring for him, Mark would be heading for the hills.

She shifted so that she was lying next to him, on her back and staring at the ceiling. By blinking very fast, she managed to keep the tears at bay. Part of her wanted to scream out against the unfairness of it all. Part of her wanted to tell him that if he was leaving he should try to keep the door from hitting him on the ass.

"I'd like to meet him."

The unexpected words hung in the room like balloons. She stopped blinking. A single tear slipped out of the corner of her eye and ran toward her temple.

"What?"

Mark leaned over her. "I said I would like to meet your brother. Why are you crying?"

She sniffed. "I'm not."

"I saw a tear."

"I have something in my eye."

"Liar." He spoke the word gently, then brushed her mouth with his. "I mean it, Darcy. I would like to meet Dirk. Unless you think it would be too weird for him."

She didn't know what to say. No one had ever wanted to meet Dirk before. She'd learned to stop expecting that kind of miracle.

She gazed at Mark's face and reminded herself that this man might look pretty amazing on the outside, but on the inside, he still didn't trust women very much. She had to make sure she didn't fall in love with him.

"It's a long drive," she said, trying to give him an out in case he'd just been being polite.

"I know where the Madison School is. Are you trying to tell me you don't want me to meet him?"

"No. I just—" She smiled. "I'm going next Saturday. You're welcome to join me."

"I'd like that."

"Move them to the right," Darcy called. "Santa has to be centered."

Josh glowered at her from his place on the roof. "Is this where I remind you that I'm doing this as a favor to a friend. I'm not getting paid and I don't care if Santa is centered or straight or even up. It's cold and I'm hungry."

Darcy smiled. "I'm sorry, Josh. Did you say something?"

Josh turned his attention to Mark. "You should be able to talk some sense into her."

"You'd think, but you'd be wrong."

Mark chuckled as his friend straightened the plastic Santa covered in lights, all the while grumbling about people being perfectionists over the stupidest things. He thought about explaining that he hadn't exactly tap-danced at the thought of spending an evening in the frigid night air hanging lights and putting up Christmas decorations, but Darcy had asked him to help and he'd been unable to refuse her. The fact that his ankle wasn't a hundred percent meant that he'd had to call in reinforcements.

He finished stapling the white lights around the porch about the same time Josh climbed down off the roof. Darcy eyed their work critically.

"Very nice," she said.

Mark joined her, limping only slightly. It was Wednesday. His ankle had continued to hurt through Monday but then had started to heal. He rested his weight on his good leg and resisted the urge to put his arm around Darcy. Since they'd had their heart-to-heart talk, they'd been spending their evenings together, although not their nights. Mark wasn't sure he was ready to be back in her bed. Something profound had happened the last time they'd been intimate.

Somehow, sharing his past and hearing more about her brother had changed things. It was as if in the telling of their secrets, they'd shifted their relationship. He didn't want to think about what that meant. Trust still wasn't easy for him. He'd been completely wrong about Sylvia, and while that didn't mean he couldn't be right about Darcy, he wanted to be sure. There was no way he was going to make another mistake like that one.

Darcy snuggled close, wrapping her arms around him as she gazed at the duplex. "Does it make you believe in miracles?"

"We must not be looking at the same thing."

He saw a slightly tired building with half outlined in white lights. A flashing Santa sat above the center of the porch. No doubt she saw a wonderland.

"Don't be cynical," she told him. "You both did a great job. I really appreciate it."

"Yeah, well, you're welcome," Josh muttered ungraciously. "Now I'm going home before I freeze to death."

"Do you want to come inside first?" Darcy asked. "I feel badly making you do work and then sending you off on an empty stomach. I have carrot cake."

Josh laughed. "Darcy, you already gave me two dozen cookies and a pumpkin loaf. I don't need anything else."

"Are you sure?"

"Positive." Josh gave them a wave and headed for his truck.

Mark stared after him. If Darcy had her way, she would feed the world.

"I know you won't turn down my carrot cake," she said, moving toward the house.

"You're right on that."

Five minutes later he dug his fork into a large piece of cake. One bite told him that Darcy had made this as well as she made everything else.

"It's great," he said when he'd swallowed.

She poured him a cup of coffee. "I'm glad you like it. I think the tofu blends nicely with the other flavors."

He had another forkful halfway to his mouth. At her words, he froze. "No way."

She blinked innocently. "Way."

"You didn't put tofu in here."

Her smile gave nothing away.

Cautiously he took another bite. It still tasted heavenly. The cake was moist, the frosting just sweet enough to make his mouth water.

"Hell, if this is tofu, sign me up," he muttered in defeat.

Darcy dropped a kiss on his cheek. "I wish I could say it was. I'm just having a good time at your expense."

"It's not politically correct to take advantage of a man when he's injured."

"On the contrary, this is the only time I get a chance to best you."

She walked over to the counter and started pulling ingredients out of the cupboard.

"What are you making tonight?" he asked.

"More sugar cookies. Melissa doubled her order today. She said they're selling a lot faster than she thought. And I have to make gingerbread for another house. The hospital said they wanted to raffle one off at their Christmas party on Friday. I'll get it baked and cut out tonight, then assemble it tomorrow."

As she spoke, her shoulders drooped with weariness.

"How late are you going to be up tonight?" he asked.

"I don't want to think about it."

"Can I help? If you mixed up the gingerbread here, we could bake it at my place. That would free you up to concentrate on the cookies."

She gave him a grateful smile. "Are you sure you don't mind?"

"Not at all."

"Thanks."

She collected large mixing bowls and baking pans for the gingerbread, then shooed him off to preheat his oven. As Mark made his way to his own place, he wondered if she would accept money from him. He had some put away. He could help her pay for the next semester of Dirk's schooling.

But even as he came up with the plan, he dismissed it. Darcy would never take that kind of help. Using his oven was one thing, but money was something else. She was stubborn and proud.

She was also everything he'd wanted Sylvia to be.

The difference was Darcy was the genuine article. So what exactly did he want from her?

Their relationship wasn't like any he'd had before. With Sylvia there'd been sudden, overwhelming attraction. He'd been smitten from the second he'd seen her. With Darcy, things had happened more slowly. Although not sexually, he reminded himself with a grin as he walked into his kitchen and turned on the oven. The physical chemistry between them was the most powerful he'd ever experienced. But the rest of it—the friendship or whatever he wanted to call it—had been slow in growing. Like a tiny ember that grew to be a—

A what? Forest fire? He shook his head. That was too big. That implied a kind of connection that made him uncomfortable. He and Darcy weren't in love, they were—

He paused again, trying to define their relationship, all the while hating his own indecision. Before Sylvia, he'd always known where he stood with the women in his life. Usually they didn't engage him. Sylvia had seemed like the answer to his prayers. So what was Darcy?

"Bigger is better," Darcy said the next evening as they stood freezing in the Christmas tree lot. "I want it to fill the living room."

Mark stared at the monstrosity she'd picked. "If you get this one it *will* fill the living room, because it's too tall. You'd either have to cut it in half or turn it on its side."

"You think?" She tilted her head to gaze up at the

gorgeous tree she'd chosen. "It's just that I usually don't have a very big budget for decorating. But this year, with all the extra money from my baking, I thought I'd go a little wild."

"I suggest going wild on a smaller scale."

She thought about the low ceilings in her duplex and sighed. "I guess you're right. I don't want to have to cut the tree to make it fit. So if we can't get a tall one, let's get a really bushy one."

"There won't be room to sit anywhere."

She laughed. "Aren't you Mr. Crabby Pants? Mark, it's Christmas. You need to get into the spirit."

Instead of answering, he took her hand and led her to a different section of the lot. Once there he started talking about different kinds of trees. As she didn't know Douglas fir from cat fur, she didn't pay attention to what he was saying. Instead she allowed herself to get caught up in the play of light on his handsome features and the way he gestured when he spoke.

She liked that, even though he wasn't much of a holiday guy, he was earnestly trying to make sure she got the right tree for her place. Not that he would buy one for himself.

"Are you sure you don't want a tree?" she asked, interrupting him.

Mark sighed in frustration. "Yes, I'm sure. I don't do trees. If I get a burning urge to participate in the holiday spirit, I'll come over to your place."

"What about a little one for your table."

"Darcy!"

"Okay. Fine. I'll get a tree. But you can pick it out so that it feels more like your own."

An hour later they were back in her living room. Mark had put the massively fat tree into the stand and was positioning it as much in the corner as possible.

"We're going to have to move the sofa," he told her.

She ignored his "I told you so" expression. "That's not a problem. I'll just pull it toward the dining room."

"You'll have to climb over it to get down the hall."

She glanced at the sofa, then at the entrance to the tiny hallway that led to her bedroom and the bathroom. "If we put it at an angle…"

"Then there's no room for the coffee table."

She smiled. "It's Christmas, Mark. We can do without a coffee table."

He grumbled under his breath, then obligingly carried the table into the dining room. Through a bit of shifting and pushing, they managed to fit the sofa and the chair and the tree all into the living room. The scent of pine drifted through the apartment. Darcy carried in the boxes of ornaments she'd had stored in the garage.

"Some of these are from when I was a little girl," she said, setting the boxes down on the sofa and opening the top one. "I made a few of them myself, so don't laugh."

"I'd never laugh at you."

His words made her shiver. Darcy didn't dare turn around and look at Mark. Not when she was afraid of what he would see in her eyes. There was something magical about spending this holiday with him. She didn't know what was going to happen between them—she still didn't know how to define their relationship. All she knew was that when she was with him, she felt really good inside.

"Will you see your sister for the holidays?" she asked, digging around for lights. She found the first string and handed it to Mark.

"No. Maddie's going to be on the road. What about you? Will you go see Dirk? Or will he come here?"

"I'll go there on Christmas Day. There's a big celebration at the school. Apparently a lot of parents and family come. I'm looking forward to it. I have to work the week between Christmas and New Year's. We discussed Dirk coming here for a few days, but as he'd be alone most of the day, he said he would rather stay at school."

She hesitated, torn between wanting to invite Mark to join them for Christmas and wondering if that was too presumptuous. He was already meeting Dirk in a few days. Would he really want more contact with her brother? And yet if she didn't invite him, was she being rude?

"What about Christmas Eve?" he asked.

She handed him more lights. But instead of taking them from her, he grabbed her hand.

"Darcy?"

She looked at him. He smiled.

"Would you please spend Christmas Eve with me?" he asked. "We can open our presents."

Her heart thundered in her chest and her mouth went dry. ''Presents?''

''Just a couple of little things to make you smile.''

He was getting her presents? Something worth smiling over? Her brain instantly flashed to an engagement ring. In that same instant, she told herself not to be silly. Mark wasn't going to propose to her.

Her legs gave way and she plopped onto the sofa.

''Hey, are you all right?'' he asked.

''Fine. Christmas Eve would be great.''

Did her voice sound okay? Could he hear the terror in her voice. Terror that came not from fear that he would propose—but fear that he wouldn't. She realized in that second, she wanted him to. Because she'd fallen in love with him.

Chapter Thirteen

"So the thing is I've never brought anyone to see Dirk before," Darcy said. "I don't know what he's going to think or say. I know we're friends, but you're also a guy and that could have an impact on him."

"You think?" Mark asked calmly, never taking his attention from the road.

Darcy nodded even though he couldn't see her movement. "Sure. I mean Dirk has some developmental issues, but he's also a fourteen-year-old boy. There are hormones at work. Not that he's shown any interest in the whole boy-girl thing. I don't even want to think about that. Talk about a nightmare in the making. My point is—"

Mark spared her a quick smile. "Darcy, I know what your point is. Dirk may be completely fine with meeting me. He may also be threatened. I won't take it personally if it's the latter. I promise to do my best to make him like me. Now would you please calm down before you give yourself a heart attack?''

"I'm fine."

"No, you're not. If you bounce your foot any harder, you're going to break through the floor of my truck."

"What?" She glanced down at her leg. Sure enough it was jumping around as she gave in to her nervousness. "I might be a little tense," she admitted. "It's just I've never done anything like this before."

"Everything is going to be fine," he promised.

Easy for him to say, she thought to herself. What he didn't know was that she had a lot more on the line that he realized. She desperately wanted things to go well with Dirk. If she had any chance at a long-term relationship with Mark, he was going to have to get along with her brother. And figuring out that she was in love with Mark had made her want things to last as long as possible.

She still couldn't believe she'd fallen for him, but given what they'd been through together, she shouldn't be surprised. There had to be a reason that she'd ended five years of celibacy with him. Some of it was sexual chemistry, but some of it was something much more. She was drawn to his strength—both physical and emotional. She liked who he was and how he lived his life. She admired him. And there was the small detail of him being easy on the eye and darned good in bed. What was there not to like?

The question was—should she tell him about her feelings? So far every fiber of her being had screamed "no" really loud. The man had recently been through a horrible experience with a woman he'd wanted to marry. She wasn't completely sure he was over that. Or if he was, she could be his rebound relationship. Neither possibility gave her any reason to put her heart on the line.

They pulled into the parking lot of the school before she had a chance to calm herself. In what felt like seconds, they'd made their way to the great room, where Dirk was waiting along with several of his school friends. She'd warned him that she was bringing a friend and now she waited anxiously to see how her brother would react.

He walked toward them slowly. Darcy's heart filled with love as she stared into her brother's familiar face. He was tall and good-looking and obviously happy. He grinned at her. She flew into his arms and they hugged. Then she stepped back and introduced them.

"Dirk, this is Mark. He lives next door to me. He's a detective."

Her brother and Mark shook hands. "Nice to meet you. Darcy's told me a lot about you," Mark said easily.

Dirk nodded. "Darcy always says nice stuff about me. A detective works with the police. Do you keep Darcy safe?"

"I work for the local sheriff's office rather than the police, which is almost the same. Do you worry about your sister?"

Dirk nodded. "She's by herself now. I don't want her to get scared at night."

"I see." He gazed at the young man. "Darcy knows that if she ever gets scared, she can call me. I'm right next door and I'll do everything I can to keep her safe."

Dirk nodded. "Good."

Darcy felt some of her apprehension fade away. She'd been worried about this meeting, but it seemed as if things might work out after all. Mark had taken Dirk's concerns seriously, while her brother didn't seem threatened by her having a man in her life.

She linked arms with both of them. "So what's on the schedule for today?" she asked.

"I want to show Mark my pictures from Chicago," Dirk said. He glanced over her head. "I went there with my school. It was Thanksgiving. We took the train and then stayed in a hotel."

"Sounds like fun," Mark said.

"It was. I took my camera. Darcy gave it to me and then she gave me film. I like taking pictures."

"He's very good at it," Darcy told Mark. She returned her attention to her brother. "Then what?"

"After lunch some of the guys want to play basketball. I'd like you to watch."

"Absolutely," she promised. "I'll even cheer when you get a basket."

Dirk smiled. "Would you like to play with us?" he asked Mark.

"It just so happens that basketball is my game."

Life was bitterly unfair, Darcy thought later that afternoon as her brother and Mark raced down the court. The two guys were a terrific twosome, tossing the ball back and forth, making baskets and then high-fiving each other. They didn't look that much alike, but there was a similarity in their physical grace.

Mark had collected his workout clothes from his gym bag in his truck. Darcy tried not to notice how good he looked sweating. She'd worried about him and Mark for no reason. They were getting along like old friends. Which made her concerned for a completely different reason. How was she supposed to resist him now?

"Darcy's got a boyfriend."

She turned toward the singsong voice and saw Andrew climbing the bleachers to sit next to her.

"I'm not even going to dignify that comment with a reply," she said with a sniff.

Andrew laughed. "Dirk told me you were bringing a friend. I wanted to check him out for myself."

"What do you think?"

He turned his attention to the basketball game. "Aside from favoring one leg, I would say he's a pretty good player."

She glared at the counselor. "He hurt himself playing last weekend, and you know that's not what I meant. I don't care about his physical prowess on the basketball court."

Andrew nodded. "I know. I watched him at lunch. He's okay with the kids. Some people feel uncomfortable, but they get over it. Others never fit in. They're awkward and find excuses to stay away. Your friend there—" he jerked his chin toward the court "—is one of the good ones. He doesn't really care that these kids are different."

"That's what I thought, too," Darcy admitted.

"You sound like you wish it wasn't true."

"I don't, exactly. Let's just say his acceptance of Dirk complicates things."

What she wasn't about to tell Andrew is that it made her more vulnerable, which was the last thing she needed with Mark. She was already in love with him and having daydreams about happily ever after. She had to keep reminding herself that he hadn't shown any interest in a permanent relationship. Her luck in the man-woman department had been pretty lousy for years and he'd just been through a horrible experience during which the woman he'd wanted to marry had tried to kill him. Not exactly a formula for romantic bliss.

"What are you scared of?" Andrew asked.

"I'm not afraid. More resigned. Life has taught me that when things get tough, people tend to desert like rats on a sinking ship."

Andrew returned his attention to the game. Dirk made another basket and Mark yelled out congratulations.

"Maybe your friend is more the lifeboat kind."

"Maybe."

She desperately wanted to believe it, but she was afraid of being let down again. She was tired of being hurt. Not that she had much choice. Now that she was in love with him, it was unlikely she would get out of this unscathed.

"I had a good time," Mark said on their drive home. "Thanks for inviting me."

"You're welcome."

He gave her a teasing smile. "All that worry for nothing."

She nodded. "I guess I shouldn't have sweated the visit so much. Dirk really enjoyed meeting you." In fact, her brother had seemed more sad that Mark was leaving than that she was going as well.

"I liked meeting him, too. He's a special kid with a very special sister. You've done a hell of a job, Darcy."

"I don't deserve any praise."

"Sure you do. You've worked your butt off to provide for your brother. Just in the past six or eight months you've uprooted yourself, moved to an unfamiliar town and enrolled your brother in a wonderful, but very expensive school. You're strapped for cash and determined that he get the best education he can."

While she appreciated the praise, she didn't understand it. "He's my brother. What else would I have done? You took care of your sister."

"My situation wasn't anything like yours. Maddie was already in high school when our folks died and, except for the usual teenage stuff, didn't require anything extra of me. You took on taking care of Dirk when a lot of more prepared people would have walked away. And you've helped me a lot."

"Me?" She turned toward him. "What are you talking about?"

"I came back to Whitehorn physically on the mend, but the rest of me was a mess. I hadn't worked through all my conflicting emotions about Sylvia. I wasn't ready to be back in the world. I wanted to hide and lick my wounds. You got in the way of that. I owe you.''

"I was just being a friend. You don't owe me anything.''

She didn't want his gratitude or a debt. She wanted something more permanent. Hope fluttered in her chest and no matter how much she told herself it was dangerous, the light, tickly feeling wouldn't go away.

"About Christmas," he said. "You're going to spend it with Dirk?"

"Yes." She bit her lower lip. "Do you have plans?"

"Not really."

"Do you want to come with me? You don't have to," she added hastily. "I mean it's going to be a big crowd and I know that's not your thing."

"I'd like to go," he told her.

"Good."

The fluttering in her chest increased. She was sinking in fourteen kinds of trouble and didn't know how to keep herself from drowning.

"What time do you want to head to the school?" he asked.

"About nine in the morning. That will put us there around ten. They eat at two, and we can come back after dinner."

"Works for me. I'll call Maddie before we leave."

"Where is your sister?"

"Somewhere in Texas. There's a series of rodeos in the area, so she's actually settled down for a few weeks. She has a lot of friends there."

"Do you see her much?"

"No. Maddie likes to be on the rodeo circuit. For some reason she isn't one for staying in the same place."

"Was she like that as a child?"

"Some. She always loved horses."

"Unlike her older brother," Darcy teased.

"You got that right. I don't hate them, but I don't get the fascination. And why anyone would want to spend his life looking after cows is beyond me. They're stupid and they smell."

She laughed. "You're mocking one of Montana's prime industries."

He winked at her, then returned his attention to the road. "Don't get me wrong. I enjoy a decent steak as much as the next guy, but that doesn't mean I want to meet my meal on the hoof."

"It's a good thing you headed off to New York when you did," she said. "Otherwise your blasphemy would have offended the neighbors."

"Maddie rags on me all the time," he admitted. "She says that I couldn't have been born here. That our folks must have found me on the side of the road somewhere back East but were just too embarrassed to tell anyone."

Darcy laughed. "She sounds like fun. I'd like to meet her sometime."

"I wouldn't mind seeing her myself." He frowned. "It's been a while. After our parents died we clung to each other. We had a great aunt. June was an incredible woman. We thought she was about as old as the hills, but in a cool way." He shrugged. "She started visiting us. First it was for a long weekend, then for a couple of weeks. Finally, she was spending more time at our place than at hers. When I finished college, she moved in so that I could head off to New York.''

"You have some wonderful memories to counteract the bad ones.''

"I guess I do.''

She wondered if he would use her to counteract his memories of Sylvia or if she would have a place of her own.

"What happened to your house?'' she asked instead. "The one you grew up in?''

"We sold it when Aunt June died and split the money. Aunt June left us what she had. I gave that all to Maddie to buy her truck and trailer, along with the gear she needed for her rodeo career.''

"It sounds like you two had to grow up fast, too,'' she said. "Losing significant people has a way of doing that.''

"It taught me to be self-sufficient,'' Mark said. "I regret the losses but not the lessons.''

She'd learned something different, Darcy thought sadly. Instead of being autonomous, she wanted to belong—to be a part of something bigger than herself. She doubted that Mark shared her desire for home and hearth—a family. He'd already learned his lesson on that one.

Christmas Eve was perfect. The night was cold and clear, with a promise of new snow for Christmas morning. The dinner had turned out well, although

there was enough ham left over to feed half of Whitehorn. Now she and Mark cuddled together on the
sofa, staring at her perfect tree, watching the lights
twinkle in the semidarkness.

"That tree needs to go on a diet," Mark said.

"And here I was thinking this was a perfect moment," she complained. "The tree is not fat. It's a
little broad through the base is all."

"It's pear shaped."

Darcy squinted at the tree. Okay, so there was a
disproportionate amount of branches at the bottom.
Still it was her tree and she loved it.

"If you'd let me get the really tall one, you
wouldn't be complaining that the tree was fat."

He kissed her lightly. "If I'd let you get the tall
one, we would have had to put it outside to make it
fit. It would have made decorating it a cold proposi-
tion."

Darcy opened her mouth, then closed it. She'd
started to tell him that next time he could pick. She
bit back the words, not knowing if there was going
to *be* a next time. She wanted there to be. She
couldn't imagine herself loving anyone else the way
she loved him.

"Come on," he said, slipping off the sofa and settling on the ground in front of the tree. "Let's open
presents."

"Okay."

Darcy sat crossed-legged next to him, trying not to
feel too nervous. She hadn't ever bought a man a
present before. The goofy gifts she'd given boyfriends
in high school and college didn't seem to count. She'd

thought for a long time, not sure what Mark would like. Her first idea had been something to spruce up his bare apartment, but that had seemed too impersonal.

Mark sorted through the packages. She'd been eyeing the big box he'd brought over with some trepidation. It was the size of a large laundry basket, but she didn't think that would be his idea of a gift.

"I see several for Dirk," he said. "What did you get him?"

"One of those robot dogs." She laughed. "I'm sure it's going to make everyone at the school crazy. Apparently it barks when it's excited and whimpers when it's lonely. It has to be fed."

He looked at her. "What do we feed a fake dog?"

"Some kind of fake bone." She shrugged. "According to the guy at the store, the dog can be programmed to recognize a voice and even do tricks. It will take some work, but when I talked to Andrew, he felt it would be good for Dirk. Not only fun, but it will help him read and follow directions. I also got him a remote control car, some videos and a gift certificate for clothes. The school suggested that so they can take the students shopping and teach them to make good choices on their own."

Mark stared at her. "I didn't realize that buying for Dirk was so complicated." He looked uncomfortable. "I just got him a new basketball."

Darcy hadn't realized that one of the presents from Mark had been for Dirk. His thoughtfulness overwhelmed her. Tears sprang to her eyes. She threw her arms around him and held him close.

"Hey," he said lightly. "It wasn't all that big a deal."

"Yes it was." She sniffed. "I didn't expect you to get him anything. You took time out of your busy schedule to get something special for my brother. That means a lot to me."

He hugged her. Darcy savored the feel of his body next to hers. Although they'd been spending a lot of time together, they hadn't been making love. She didn't know what that meant and did her best not to think about it. In many ways her relationship with Mark was entirely too complicated, although very wonderful.

She straightened and wiped away any trace of tears. "Okay. Enough foolishness. Show me the loot."

Mark chuckled. He pulled the large mystery box toward him, then set it in front of her.

"Here's the thing," he said. "I really wrestled with this one."

She eyed the box. "Is it a bear?"

"Not that kind of wrestling. I didn't know if I should get this or not. It's one of those practical presents. I know that women have a thing about that. But I did it because I worry about you and I wanted to make your life easier."

"Is it a muffler for my car?"

"Would you just open it?"

She stared at the Santa paper and the crooked seams of the wrapping. The bow was off center and Mark had used enough tape to hold together a ship. She thought the package looked wonderful.

But what had he gotten her? She ripped paper off

one side of the box. It was just a white shipping box and the plain cardboard didn't give any hints. She quickly tore the rest of it away, then pried open the top.

Inside were packing peanuts and something large and flat. She pulled out an expensive two-layer cookie sheet, then glanced at Mark.

He looked vaguely uncomfortable. "If you're going to be spending all your time in the kitchen, I thought you might like to be working with something better than those old pans of yours." He hesitated. "I wasn't sure because there are all those horror stories about insensitive men buying blenders for gifts. I didn't mean it like that."

Darcy stared at the label on the pan. It was high-end stuff. More than she could afford, even on her best day. Judging from the weight of the box, it wasn't the only one inside.

"You can't buy these here."

"I know. I found a place on-line and got it through them."

She dropped the pan and threw her arms around him. "Thank you. They're wonderful."

"You're not mad?"

"Not even a little. I think they're fabulous."

The tingling was back, along with hope for their future. Mark hadn't gotten her something easy and generic. He'd put a lot of effort into the bakeware. Maybe she did matter to him after all.

He kissed her. "There's more than just the one cookie sheet. You could look at the rest of them."

He sounded like a little kid who wanted his school

project admired. She returned to the box and drew out three more cookie sheets and two sets of cake pans. There were also four loaf pans and a specially designed multilayer cooling rack. Talk about a fantasy collection.

"I'm impressed," she said. "Thank you. I mean it."

"Good."

She sat on her heels and handed him a box. Shopping for him had been challenge. Not only was there the issue of her budget, but what exactly was she supposed to get for a man who didn't seem to need or want anything?

Mark opened the box and pulled out a sweater. It was hand-knit, thick and in multiple shades of green blended with black. It had cost her a chunk of change plus two gingerbread houses.

"It's perfect," he said, holding it up to himself. "Am I stylish?"

"Always." She touched the wool. "Do you like it? I had it made because I'm hopeless with knitting and sewing. I know it's clothes, which isn't a guy thing, but I thought..."

Now it was his turn to hug her. "I'm not kidding, Darcy. I really do like it. I'll wear it tomorrow when we go see your brother."

"I'd like that."

Darcy's expression was so hopeful, Mark found himself willing to walk through fire rather than disappoint her. At least she hadn't thought his present was stupid. He'd been worried that she wouldn't understand that he was trying to help. But even as they sat together, she kept glancing at the pans as if he'd given her an unexpected treasure. Based on what she'd told him about her life, he would bet that it had been a long time since someone had bothered to pay attention to her needs.

He found himself wanting to step into the role. Being around her made him feel as if he belonged— possibly for the first time in years. Funny how he'd been so sure he was in love with Sylvia, yet he'd never relaxed around her. With Darcy he could be himself.

"I have something else for you," she said, handing him a flat box that felt exactly like a book.

He opened the package. It was a book. One on dealing with and preventing sports injuries. He chuckled. "Gee, thanks. Is this a statement on my physical prowess?"

"Uh-huh." She laughed.

He handed her a small box. She opened in. Inside were a dozen lottery tickets, all from different states.

"A buffet of possibilities," he teased. "One of those might be worth millions. Or at least thousands."

She fingered the tickets. "At this point in time I would be excited by fifty dollars. Want to open them now?"

"If you'd like. Or we could have pie."

She tucked the lottery tickets back in the box and put them under the tree. "Far be it from me to stand between a man and his pumpkin pie. This way, sir."

He followed her into the kitchen. This had been the best Christmas he'd had in recent memory. There was a message in that information. Perhaps it was time for him to pay attention to it.

Two days after Christmas, Melissa North held open the front door to her house. "Thanks for coming out on such short notice," she said as Mark stepped into the foyer.

"Not a problem."

He followed her into her western-style living room and settled on the sofa. Melissa sat opposite in a club chair. She wore her dark hair pulled away from her face. Her fingers were restless on her lap and there was an edge of worry in her expression.

"I was speaking with the sheriff yesterday. He says you haven't found any evidence of money laundering at my café."

Melissa owned the Hip Hop. Mark flipped through his notes. "We've come up with exactly zero. I'm meeting with Rafe later today. We're going to pool information and figure what, if anything, we know. As far as I can tell, all your employees are clean."

She sighed. "That's good to know. I'd been worried because I consider myself a good judge of character. It would be disconcerting to suddenly be proved wrong."

She stopped talking and stared at him. Mark didn't say anything. There was something about her body language that told him she'd had another reason for asking him to stop by. Experience had taught him that silence was a persuasive tool for getting people to speak.

"I don't even know if I should mention this," she said after a couple of minutes. "It sounds so stupid."

"I live for stupid," he said easily. "I promise not to laugh."

She shook her head. "I'm sure it's nothing, but it's weird and kind of creepy."

Mark didn't like the sound of that. "What is weird and creepy?"

"I've been getting hang-up calls. At first I thought it was someone with a wrong number, but it doesn't feel like that. I know that doesn't make sense."

Mark wrote on his pad. "I've learned to trust people's gut feelings about this sort of thing. Anything else?"

She paused before speaking. "I found a dead bird on the welcome mat. I don't think it died there. It's almost as if someone is sending me a message. But I don't know what it means."

"Do you and your husband have any enemies?" Mark asked. "People who want to get you back for something?"

"No. I've been trying to think of anyone who would want to make trouble for me. I haven't even fired anyone. My last few employees left because they wanted to. And Wyatt, my husband, can't think of anyone, either."

Mark didn't like the sound of the calls or the dead bird.

"I'll ask around," he told her. "If I hear anything, I'll let you know. Start keeping a log of your hang-up calls. If you get more than a couple more, we'll go to the phone company and get a trace put on your line. If anything else strange happens, page me. Don't hesitate, even if it's the middle of the night.''

"Okay. Thanks.''

Mark rose and left. He'd returned to Montana expecting to find life pretty boring. First Darcy had come into his world and now this. Was it possible there was going to be trouble in Whitehorn?

Chapter Fourteen

Mark left Melissa North's house and drove directly to the sheriff's office. Rafe was in, talking on the phone as Mark tapped on his open door. The other man waved him in. Mark took a seat and flipped through his notes until Rafe hung up the phone.

"What's up?" the sheriff asked.

Mark crossed his leg, resting his ankle on his opposite knee. "A couple of things. I've been through the backgrounds of every employee at the Hip Hop Café, including that of Janie and Melissa North, who owns the place. I can't come up with a single lead."

Rafe dug through several files on his desk. The dark-haired sheriff pulled one out and opened it. "I have the report back from the forensic accountant. There's a job we should all have," he said with a grin.

''Not me.''

''Yeah, I was never a numbers person, either. Anyway she's been through the Hip Hop's books front to back. She came up with nada.''

Mark wasn't surprised. ''So we're at a dead end.''

''Do you think the phone call was a hoax?''

Mark shrugged. ''I don't know how else to explain it. The problem is, why do it in the first place? It's not the sort of thing kids would do. If it's not true, who else would bother?''

Rafe frowned. ''I see what you mean. Teenagers tend to go for splashier crimes. It's one thing to steal a car for a joy ride. There's the thrill of breaking the law and showing off to friends. But this isn't their style. So who else had something to gain by sending us on a wild-goose chase?''

''That's what doesn't make sense. Okay, so we wasted a bunch of time. So what? It's not as if there were more pressing crimes that went without an investigation. If this were a bigger city, I would say we'd been had by a crazy person. The only person who fits that description is Homer Gilmore. He talks to himself, but I can't see him doing this, can you?''

''No.'' Rafe leaned back in his chair. ''Well, Mark, it looks like we have ourselves a bona fide mystery. Think we're going to solve it?''

''No. And there's more. I went to see Melissa North today. She wanted to know how the money laundering investigation was going. While I was there she told me that she's been having hang-up calls. Someone also left a dead bird on her doorstep.''

Rafe swore. ''What the hell is going on here? This

is Whitehorn. We're not supposed to have serious crime here.''

"I don't know if it's serious or not. I told Melissa to keep track of the next few hang-ups. If they continue, we'll need to put a tracer on the phone line." He patted his belt. "I also told her to page me with any information or questions.''

Rafe grinned. "About time someone got you out of bed in the middle of the night. The department paid good money for that pager.''

"Because Whitehorn is so big, you wouldn't know where to find me?''

Rafe's humor faded. "I don't like any of this," he admitted.

"I agree. I've got a bad feeling. Plus I can't help thinking that I'm missing something really important. It's just out of reach.''

"Let me know when you figure it out.''

"If I do." Mark rose. "See you tomorrow, boss.''

"Later,'' Rafe said, just as his phone rang.

Mark returned to his office. There weren't that many people around—the week between Christmas and New Year's was traditionally slow. He plowed through paperwork until his eyes burned, then headed for home.

The duplex was dark when he pulled up. Darcy had a rare dinner shift and wouldn't be home until later. He let himself into his place, only to stand in his empty living room and wish he could be next door with her. He wanted to curl up with her on her sofa, admiring her fat Christmas tree and eating something that she'd baked. He wanted to listen to her laughter, get lost in her conversation and try to talk himself out of making love with her.

Despite the fact that he'd avoided her bed for the past week or so, he hadn't stopped wanting her. In fact he wanted her more than he ever had. But something had changed between them and until he figured out what it was, he planned on staying clear of the sensual playground that was making love with Darcy.

He flicked on lights, then headed for the kitchen and grabbed a beer. Maybe he should have stopped at the Hip Hop for dinner. At least then he could have seen Darcy.

He leaned against the counter and took a long drink. He was home now. Instead of heading back out, he'd wait for her to return. Knowing her, she would probably bring him leftovers. They'd eat them together. Then—

He paced restlessly. Then, what? He walked the length of his living room before returning to the dining room. He had too many questions and no answers. Darcy was an amazing woman. She'd managed to keep herself and her brother afloat financially for the past five years. He knew she worried about Dirk. While her brother would eventually be able to be on his own in the world, he would never be a hundred percent self-sufficient. Someone would always need to be nearby. That person was going to be Darcy.

Whoever was in her life would be signing up for more than the usual responsibilities.

Mark turned that thought over in his mind. Was the reality of her situation enough to scare him away, or did he think it wouldn't be such hard duty? He liked Dirk—the kid was a lot of fun. What would it be like when that kid was a forty-year-old man? What about if Dirk wanted to get married and have children?

Mark waited for his gut to tell him to head for the hills. He didn't need that kind of trouble. And yet he knew the restlessness he felt inside had nothing to do with wanting to avoid Darcy and her situation. If anything he felt compelled to offer a strong shoulder. Shared burdens were always easier.

He walked to the window and stared out at the lightly falling snow. At one time he would have reminded himself that he'd already been down this road and it was way too dangerous to tread. But he'd learned his lesson. Darcy wasn't Sylvia. She never had been. Darcy was the most honest, trustworthy person he knew.

He'd made one really big mistake. Both he and Sylvia had paid for it. Maybe it was time to let the past go. The future was far more important. *Darcy* was more important.

In his previous relationship, he'd felt a flash of emotion. Something hot and immediate had convinced him Sylvia was the one. He hadn't felt that with Darcy. Oh, there'd been plenty of sexual combustion, but his heart had been slower to engage.

His feelings had grown slowly. Cautious liking, turning to respect and affection. And now...

Now he didn't know. He cared about Darcy a lot. He wanted her in his life. Did that make his feelings real? Did he love her? Did he want forever?

* * *

Darcy arrived home with a bag full of leftovers and sore feet. She hadn't been scheduled to go in until two, but one of the waitresses had called in sick, so she'd been at the Hip Hop since eight that morning. A thirteen-hour shift wasn't her idea of a good time.

As she pulled into her carport, she saw lights on in Mark's place and his silhouette in the front window. Before she'd done more than turn off the engine, he was at her door, opening it and pulling her into a hug.

"I missed you," he said, then kissed her with an intensity that left her breathless.

She responded, hoping that she could persuade him to take her to bed. She wasn't the least bit sleepy, but she could sure do with an hour or two of incredible lovemaking. But instead of taking the hint, he took a step back and inhaled.

"Do I smell fried chicken?"

"Absolutely. It was the special tonight. I brought mashed potatoes and green beans, too." She gave him a mock glare to cover her disappointment that once again he wasn't interested in physical intimacy.

"I can't wait." He leaned over and grabbed the bags on the passenger seat, then closed the door and put his arm around her. They walked into her apartment.

Twenty minutes later they'd eaten most of the chicken and potatoes. Darcy pushed the container of green beans toward Mark.

"Two tablespoons' worth isn't a serving."

"It is to me."

"You'll get scurvy."

"I take a multivitamin every morning."

"Is this before or after you clog your arteries with your heart-attack-inducing breakfast?"

"Before." He gave her a smile that showed no remorse. "I'm changing the subject. How was your day?"

"Long. Janie called me in at eight because they were shorthanded. My feet hurt."

"I'll bet. I didn't know you'd been there that long."

"The good news is that I got overtime today. Janie felt so bad that I don't have to go in until ten, but she'll pay me for my usual time. So that will help." Darcy nibbled on a piece of chicken. "I really like my job. The people are good and the tips add up. But I hate working nights. I'm glad it's not my regular shift. Closing up a restaurant takes a lot of time. I'd much rather open."

"Were you the last one there?"

She nodded. "One of the busboys was supposed to stay and help me, but he had a hot date so I let him go early."

"I think I've just been insulted," Mark told her.

Darcy didn't get it. "How?"

"You let that other guy go early because he had a hot date. What am I? Chopped liver?"

She forced herself to smile because that's what he expected. Great joke. Life was a laugh a minute. But suddenly she felt like crying. Logic told her that she and Mark hadn't been together for very long. Neither of them was willing to define their relationship, so she didn't know if they were still friends or had moved on to something more. If she was the least bit brave, she would ask. The thing was—she didn't want to hear the answer. Not if it was bad.

"You're completely hot," she said at last. "However, we're older and I figured we would have the patience to wait to see each other."

She shifted in her seat. Everything hurt. Part of her wanted to ask Mark for a massage. However the thought of his hands on her body sent her thoughts in a direction that was far from medicinal. Besides, if he wasn't interested in her that way, she was hardly going to force things. Maybe he was getting tired of her. Maybe—

She shook her head to clear it of all those negative thoughts. "I've been cooped up inside for too long," she said impulsively. "Do you want to take a drive? It's still snowing, but there are patches of clearing and the stars look amazing tonight."

"Great idea. You bundle up and I'll go warm the truck cab."

He helped her clear the table, then left. Darcy quickly changed into jeans and a warm sweater, then pulled on her parka. Mark had parked in front of her place and was waiting when she closed and locked her front door.

"Where to?" he asked as she slid onto the bench seat.

"It's your town. You pick."

He grinned. "I know a great lookout place. We used to go park there in high school."

"Is the view nice?"

"Darcy, no one cares about the view."

Was he suggesting something? She sucked in a

breath. Lord, she hated being so conflicted about a man. "It sounds like fun," she said lightly.

"I'll take you to the best spot," he promised.

The light snow slowed as more patches of sky were visible in the parting clouds. There was a hint of moon and dozens of stars. She huddled in her jacket, waiting for the truck's heater to warm the cab.

"What are you doing for New Year's Eve?" he asked, speaking into the quiet.

"Gee, I usually have a party in Paris for a couple dozen of my closest friends. We fly over in a chartered jet and ring in the New Year with caviar and champagne."

He glanced at her. "Really? Have you ever tasted caviar? I did once. It's really salty."

"Mark!"

"Okay. So you don't have plans. Want to do something with me?"

"Yes."

She pressed her lips together. There was so much more she wanted to say. She wanted to tell him that he'd become very important to her. She wanted to ask him why he'd stopped making love with her and did he know that it was slowly killing her inside. She wanted to admit that she loved him and find out if there was a chance that he might have feelings for her as well. If he wasn't completely over Sylvia, she would wait—as long as there was a chance for them.

But she didn't say the words. For one thing, she didn't know his feelings about Dirk. Liking her brother was one thing—being willing to get involved with someone responsible for Dirk was another. Her second reason for hesitating was that she thought he would be more comfortable if he made the first move. Wasn't that how guys liked it?

If only she'd had more experience. But Mark was the first guy she'd been involved with since her folks had passed away. Her relationships in college had been so incredibly shallow that she had no way to compare them to what was currently going on in her life.

By the time they reached the overlook, the sky had nearly cleared. Mark put the truck in park but left the motor running. Heat poured out of the vents, warming her feet and legs.

"You're looking serious about something," he said, angling toward her.

"I'm just thinking."

"Does it hurt?"

She glared at him. "I'm very intelligent. Your inability to figure that out reflects badly on you, not me."

"Oh, aren't we snippy?" He grinned. "Actually I figured out that you're pretty smart. I'm smart, too."

"Really? I hadn't noticed." She pretended great interest in what was outside the passenger window.

Suddenly she felt his hand under her coat. He beelined for her side, where he started tickling her. Mark had unfastened his seat belt, but she was still trapped in hers. She squirmed but couldn't get away from his questing fingers. She shrieked and laughed.

"Stop!" she gasped.

"I have you in my clutches now," he said with

mock importance. "I will tickle you into submission."

She pushed his hands away. Without warning, he stopped. His expression softened as he stroked her cheek.

"I didn't expect you to show up," he told her. "I came home to lick my wounds and figure out what I was going to do with my life. Suddenly you were in my face, arguing with me about what I ordered for breakfast and trying to save the world."

She felt herself getting lost in his green eyes. Her heart seemed to be beating very fast as anticipation swept through her. Mark was looking at her as if she were very precious to him. As if she mattered.

"I've never met anyone like you," he admitted. "After Sylvia, I swore I'd never get burned by a woman again. I didn't want to trust anyone or get involved. But you're easy to trust. You're a good person and there aren't that many of those around."

"I'm not that good," she said. "And there are a lot of really terrific people. You just have to look to find them."

"I forgot to mention that you like to argue with me."

"I do not." She winced. "Okay, that might prove your point, but I don't think I argue."

"Uh-huh."

He moved closer, his mouth hovering inches from hers. "You confuse the hell out of me, Darcy."

"Ditto. I don't know if I'm coming or going around you."

"Which do you want it to be?"

Before she could answer, his arms came around her. He drew her close and kissed her.

The familiar warmth, the heat, the passion all combined to sweep her away. Need poured through her. Need and a sense of being where she belonged. With Mark—

A sharp sound cut through the night. Sirens.

Mark straightened and glanced out the windshield. From their place above the city they could see several fire trucks racing across town.

"It's the whole fire crew," Mark said. "I wonder what's burning." He reached for the parking brake, then glanced back at her. "I'm sorry. I know this is a mood breaker. But there have been some strange occurrences in town lately and this fire may be related. Do you mind if we check it out?"

She shook her head. Mark had gone into cop mode. There was no point in protesting his actions. Even if she convinced him to stay here, she wouldn't have his attention. The sooner they found out about the fire, the sooner they could be back in each other's arms. At least that was her fantasy.

They followed the sounds of the sirens. Eventually they were able to see the flames reaching up toward the sky. Darcy glanced around to get her bearings. Her stomach tightened as she recognized the street and the neighborhood. An awful feeling took root inside and began to grow. Mark pulled up behind the last fire truck and got out. She climbed down after him and stared at the eerie nightmare dancing toward the stars.

Horror swept over her as she watched angry fire

destroy the Hip Hop Café. They stood well away from the engulfed building, but even from this distance the heat was nearly overwhelming. With each breath, she inhaled the scent of destruction—as the café was reduced to nothing.

The sound surprised her the most. The fire roared as it consumed. Walls creaked and groaned, beams snapped, steam from the water hissed. The ceiling crashed onto the floor.

Darcy couldn't believe what was happening. Two hours ago the Hip Hop had been right where it was supposed to be and now it was disappearing before her eyes. People gathered around them, some talking quietly, others caught up in the awesome power of the flames.

Darcy wasn't sure how long she watched. Gradually the fire grew smaller. The smoke changed from dark to light as the firefighters won their battle. Eventually there was nothing left but a pile of steaming rubble.

It was only then that Darcy realized what she'd lost. Not just her baking contract, but her job. Every source of income had just gone up in flames. Tears burned in her eyes. She turned to Mark to speak with him, only to find him in conversation with the sheriff and someone from the fire department.

"I'll find out," he was saying. He glanced at her. "Darcy, were you the last person in the building?"

He asked the question casually, as if inquiring about the weather. Yet it only took a second for the meaning of his words to sink into her brain. She'd closed the restaurant. This could all be her fault!

She grabbed his coat sleeve. "Mark, I know I turned everything off. The stove, the lights. All of it. There's a checklist for closing up. I don't do it very often, so I was working from the list, not from memory."

"I know. It's all right."

She wanted to believe him, but there was something scary in his eyes. A distance.

He put his arm around her and drew her closer. Not to comfort her, she realized, but so that she could speak directly to the sheriff and fire chief.

"Tell them what happened," he said.

Darcy outlined her last hour in the restaurant. She detailed as much of what she'd done to close up as possible. Her shaking voice made the telling a little difficult, but both men were patient. They asked her a few questions, only to be interrupted by the arrival of Melissa North, the owner of the Hip Hop Café, and a firefighter carrying a charred gas can in his hand.

"It was in the alley," he said, handing it to the fire chief. "Right by the back door."

Darcy's head began to spin. Melissa gave a cry of alarm. "I don't understand," she said.

"Neither do we," the sheriff told her. "But we're going to get to the bottom of this."

He and the fire chief moved a short distance away. Darcy couldn't hear what they were saying. She turned and saw that Mark had disappeared into the milling crowd. She felt very alone.

"I'm really sorry," she forced herself to say. Her lips felt thick and it was difficult to speak. "I swear, Melissa, I didn't do anything to start this fire."

Her boss brushed away tears. "I believe you. If they've found a gas can, then it's unlikely the fire was started by an electrical short or a burner left on. I guess——" She gave a soft cry. "I guess I'm going to have to remodel after all."

A tall man appeared and put his arms around Melissa. Darcy recognized her husband, Wyatt North. He led his wife away. Darcy noticed that everyone else seemed to have a friend or loved one to lean on. Only she stood by herself.

"Ma'am, we're going to have to speak with you again."

Darcy turned and saw the fire chief. "I don't understand. About what?"

"The fire. We'll want to go over what you remember."

"But the gas can. Isn't that how it started?"

"It's too soon for us to know." He gave her a slight smile. "No one is accusing you of anything. However, we will ask you not to leave town in the next couple of days. We have a lot of information to collect."

Darcy nodded because she couldn't speak. She could barely breathe. She had no job, no baking contract, no income at all and now she was being told not to leave Whitehorn?

"How you doing?"

She turned and saw Mark. Relief swept through her. Thank God, he was still here. She reached for him, needing to feel his arms around her, offering comfort. Instead, he pressed keys into her hand.

"I've got to get into the sheriff's office," he said

absently, not even looking at her. "Take the truck and head home. I don't know when I'll be able to leave work, but I'll have someone drive me home when I can get away."

He gave her a quick, meaningless smile and disappeared into the milling crowd. Darcy was left standing alone.

Chapter Fifteen

Sheriff Rafe Rawlings arrived at Darcy's place just before nine the next morning. "Just a few simple questions," he said politely as she slipped into the front seat of his car.

She tried to tell herself that the good news was he hadn't put her in back, where the criminals sat. Nor had he slapped on handcuffs. As they drove off, she glanced back at the duplex. Mark's truck still sat in his carport. As far as she could tell, he hadn't been home all night, nor had he arrived that morning. Where was he and what was he thinking?

Three hours later she still didn't have an answer. She'd answered questions until her throat was sore. No, she hadn't seen anyone suspicious hanging around the café. Yes, she'd turned off the stove and unplugged both coffee stations before leaving. She explained about the checklist and how she'd followed it so closely because she wasn't used to closing up at night.

That statement had brought a whole new line of questioning. Why had she suddenly asked to work that night if she didn't usually. Darcy tried to stay calm.

"I didn't request the shift change. There was a whole big mess with scheduling." She cupped her hands around the coffee the sheriff's secretary had provided and tried not to wonder if her interview was being taped or recorded without her knowledge. "One of the waitresses needed time off in the afternoon for a birthday party for her daughter. Somebody on nights needed to work a morning shift. Someone else had a doctor's appointment. We all switched everything around and no one was willing to fill in at night."

She glanced at the sheriff and tried to smile. She doubted she was successful. "The people who work it, really like it. The rest of us try to avoid it. Finally I said I'd close. It doesn't happen very often and I try to cooperate so that if I ever need to change, people are willing to trade with me."

Rafe didn't look at her as he scribbled on a pad. Darcy folded her arms over her chest. While the temperature in the room felt pleasant, she was chilled all the way to her soul. Her stomach tightened every time she thought about Mark. Why hadn't she seen him? Was he really busy or was he avoiding her? She hadn't done anything wrong, but would he believe her? Did he think that once again he'd gotten involved with a criminal? Was this situation reminding him of the one with Sylvia?

The sheriff walked her through the evening again. Darcy felt exhausted. Some of it was the interview, but most of it was probably shock and the fact that she hadn't slept the previous night. No matter how many times she showered, she couldn't get the smell of smoke out of her memory.

"That's it for now," Rafe told her. "You'll be hearing from the arson investigator. He'll want to talk with you—probably later today."

She nodded. "I lost my job when the Hip Hop burned down. I won't be going anywhere."

Rafe didn't seem overly sympathetic. "One of my men will drive you home. Thank you for your time, Ms. Montague."

She thought about asking if she was now allowed to leave the city, but she didn't want to start trouble. No doubt the sheriff would want to know why. When she was up to visiting her brother, she would call the sheriff's office and make sure it was all right with them.

Mark wasn't home when Darcy was dropped off by a young deputy. She knocked on his door for several minutes, even though she knew it was pointless. His paper still lay in front of his porch.

She grabbed it, then headed for her own place. After fixing coffee, she sat down at the table to distract herself with the headlines. Maybe she could even work up enough energy to look through the want ads, now that she needed a job. Anything to keep her from thinking that it had been way too long since Mark had disappeared the previous night. He'd given her his truck to get home, but he'd never said he would call. And he hadn't.

What was he thinking? Did he blame her for the fire? Had he disappeared from her life for good?

Pain stabbed through her chest. She gulped in a breath, wishing it was some medical problem that could be fixed by a pill or more exercise—only she knew it was something much harder to cure. She ached for the loss of all she'd ever wanted.

After being alone for so long, she'd finally allowed herself to get involved and fall in love with someone. After five years of struggling, she was nearly in reach of some financial peace of mind. In a matter of one evening, everything had been taken away from her.

Just to make things even worse than that, she might still be a suspect in the fire.

Her mind raced. Whitehorn wasn't a big place. Where would she find another job? What about Dirk? She had to keep him in the Madison School. There might be some financial aid. Lord knows she was more destitute now than she'd ever been. Maybe she should call Andrew and talk to him. She reached for the phone only to remember that he was on vacation the week between Christmas and New Year's.

Darcy resisted the urge to curl up in a ball. Somehow she had to find the strength to pull it all together. The past five years had taught her how to be a survivor. She would get through this and move on with her life. If that meant getting over Mark, she would do it.

But the thought of being without him hurt too much. To keep from focusing on her pain, she opened the paper and scanned the headlines. There was a picture of what was left of the Hip Hop and a long article. She read it through, at first only noticing that she wasn't listed as a suspect. Then she actually absorbed what the article said. Her mouth dropped open.

"Treasure Chest Of Gold And Jewelry Found In Café Foundation."

Darcy blinked. Gold and jewelry? In the foundation of the Hip Hop? Was it possible?

She read the article more carefully, but there weren't any more details. Just the mention that "the sheriff's office was investigating."

Where on earth had it come from? Was the treasure the reason for the fire? Had someone found out about it and been trying to steal it?

Someone who needed money?

Darcy's heart sank. She would certainly qualify under those circumstances and Mark knew it.

She wadded up the paper and tossed it across the room. She had to do something, anything, to keep herself from going crazy. She rose and headed for the living room. There were open boxes under the tree. Maybe if she straightened up, or even gave the place a good cleaning, she could keep from thinking about the disaster that was her life.

She cleared out boxes and wrapping paper, shoving everything into the large carton that had held her bakeware. As she worked, she tried not to remember how perfect Christmas Eve and Christmas Day had been. How Mark had been so generous to her and the way he'd really seemed to enjoy the time they'd spent at Dirk's school.

Her fingers closed around the small box containing the lottery tickets he'd given her. Hey, maybe one of them would be worth a million dollars and all her problems would be solved.

She dug in her pocket for a coin and sat on the sofa. After placing the tickets on the coffee table, she began to scratch off the first one.

Nothing, she thought in disgust. The second one had a prize of two dollars. She'd just cleared the first box on the third ticket—exposing a prize of a hundred thousand dollars—when the phone rang. She glanced at the ticket. A hundred grand? In what lifetime would that happen? Then she reached for the receiver.

"Hello?"

"Darcy, it's Mark."

The connection was garbled. She could barely understand the words. Even so her heart began to beat wildly as her spirits rose.

"Mark? Where are you? What's going on?"

"I'm—"

The phone line snapped and popped. She could tell he was talking, but she couldn't make out the words.

"—and I wanted to tell you goodbye."

She froze. "Goodbye?"

"Darcy, you know I have to do this. I'm sorry. I'll—"

He was gone.

She stared at the phone, then pushed frantically on the disconnect button. When that didn't work, she punched in the code to dial the number of her last call. She waited impatiently until a computerized recording said that cell phone was not currently available.

For nearly an hour she hovered by the phone, pacing, begging, praying that Mark would call back and explain. Finally she knew she couldn't keep fooling herself. She might not have heard everything he said, but she'd heard enough. He'd wanted to tell her goodbye. Because he'd decided to end things with her.

She sank onto the sofa and buried her face in her hands. What had made him walk away from her? The fire? Did he really think she was responsible? He couldn't. What would she have to gain by burning down the Hip Hop? The fire had left her with no job and no baking contract. What was he thinking? Or wasn't he? Was he just reacting, the way he had about the money laundering?

Or was it worse than that? Had he realized she was now destitute and still had to pay for her brother's schooling? Did he not want to be bothered with someone in trouble? Or was it that he'd never really cared about her? Had she just been fooling herself into thinking that she was more than cheap, easy sex?

Tears spilled from her eyes. She gave in to the loneliness and pain, sobbing until her throat hurt. She cried for all the time she'd spent alone and how she'd tried to do everything right, only to end up where she'd started. Abandoned and broke.

"No!" she said aloud, then sniffed. "I won't wallow in self-pity. It doesn't change anything and it only saps my strength."

She slapped her hands on the coffee table and sent

the lottery tickets flying. She gazed at the one for two dollars. Like that would help. She crumpled the one that hadn't had a prize, then idly scratched the ticket with the hundred-thousand-dollar square exposed. The next square matched.

Darcy gasped. No way, she thought. She needed three matching to win. There was not going to be another hundred-thousand-dollar square. Life wasn't that easy.

She moved the coin back and forth. Two dollars. Ten dollars. Fifty dollars.

One hundred thousand dollars.

She dropped the coin and stood up so suddenly she felt faint. She couldn't believe it. A hundred thousand dollars? Had she really won that?

She screamed out loud. She was saved! With that kind of money she could pay for Dirk's schooling, put money in the bank and not have to worry. She could work to support herself without sweating her bills every month. She could—

She paused in mid happy-dance. Her shoulders slumped and the dark cloud returned. This wasn't her money. Mark had given her the ticket, but he wouldn't have if he'd known what it was worth. She couldn't keep it. Not with how things had ended. She didn't want money from him. It was too much like being paid for services rendered.

Darcy left for the sheriff's office shortly after eight the next morning. She still hadn't slept and she felt like roadkill. It had taken her hours to compose a note to tuck in with the ticket. She'd wanted to say the right thing without giving away how much Mark had hurt her. She'd tried for flip but was afraid she'd simply come off as bitchy. So be it, she told herself as she drove through town. He could think ill of her if he liked. The bottom line was she was giving him a hundred thousand dollars.

When she reached the sheriff's office, she asked after Mark but was told he was out of town. She left the sealed envelope with the desk clerk, then returned home. Today she would start looking for work, she told herself. She would also begin the process of finding another steady baked-goods customer. There were other restaurants in town. Maybe even a coffee shop in a business office. Or what about selling things in a kiosk at the mall? She would make a few calls, then prepare some samples. If she—

Darcy turned into her driveway. She jammed on the brakes when she saw someone sitting on her front step. Someone who looked familiar.

Slowly she eased forward, then stopped in front of the duplex and turned off her car. She got out, not sure she could believe her eyes.

"Mark?"

He rose and smiled at her. Some of the pain in her heart eased a little. This was not the smile of a man who had moved on.

"You make me crazy," he said by way of greeting. He approached her, stopping when he was in front of her. "I tried to explain everything yesterday, but I was in a bad area for my cell phone and when we got cut off, I couldn't get you back."

"I know. I tried calling you."

He cupped her face in his large, strong hands. "I only have a minute. I'm still tracing the gold and jewelry found in the foundation of the Hip Hop and I have to get back to that. But I wanted to make sure we were okay."

"Are we?"

He leaned close and kissed her. "This isn't the way I planned this, Darcy, but I can't wait any longer. I love you. I've loved you for a long time, but I didn't realize it. I was too busy worrying about you being too like Sylvia and being determined never to trust again to realize what a prize you are. But I've learned my lesson. You're the most incredible woman I've ever known. I want us to live our lives together. I want to have kids with you and make a home. I tried to tell you the other night, but the fire got in the way. I'm sorry."

Her mind spun as his words washed over her, healing wounds and making her laugh with happiness. She wrapped her arms around him and held him close.

"Tell me again," she whispered.

"I love you. I want to be with you always. I want to help with Dirk and buy a house together and invite people with no families to join us for every Thanksgiving, because leading with your heart is what you do best."

She stepped back and stared at him. "So you don't think I had anything to do with the fire?"

"Never. Darcy, is that what you thought?"

She bit her lip. "I was worried about it," she admitted. "You disappeared and then that phone call."

"Never," he repeated, and kissed her. "You're the best person I know. I love you."

"I love you, too." She kissed him back, then pulled away. "However, you do realize I don't currently have a job."

He groaned. "You make me crazy. Why does that matter? We're in this together. I would like us to get married right away. Then instead of working forty-seven different jobs you can concentrate on your baking business. It's the one you like the best, isn't it?"

She nodded, still not sure this was actually happening. Mark loved her and was willing to help with her brother? Could it get any better?

She searched his face. "You believe that I love you, don't you? I mean I'm not doing this for the money."

"What money?"

"Haven't you been to your office? I left the lottery ticket there for you."

"What are you talking about?"

She couldn't believe it. "Mark, one of the tickets you gave me is worth a hundred thousand dollars. I didn't think I was entitled to the money so I returned it to you with a note. Didn't you get it?"

"I came straight here and I have to get back in about twenty minutes." He picked her up in his arms and swung her around. "So my wife is a rich woman. Cool."

She laughed and held on to him. "It's your money, not mine."

"Great. So your husband is a rich man. Either works for me." He set her on the ground. "We'll use some of it for the wedding and honeymoon, then put the rest away. Now you won't have to worry about Dirk's schooling. It's paid for.''

She kissed him. ''You're amazing,'' she whispered fiercely. ''Thank you for loving me. For understanding about my brother. Moving to Whitehorn was the best thing I ever did…for Dirk and for me.''

Mark smiled at her. ''It was a lucky break for me, too, Darcy. I've been waiting for you all my life.''

* * * * *

CALL THE ONES YOU LOVE OVER THE HOLIDAYS!

Save $25 off future book purchases when you buy any four Harlequin® or Silhouette® books in October, November and December 2001,

PLUS

receive a phone card good for 15 minutes of long-distance calls to anyone you want in North America!

WHAT AN INCREDIBLE DEAL!

Just fill out this form and attach 4 proofs of purchase (cash register receipts) from October, November and December 2001 books, and Harlequin Books will send you a coupon booklet worth a total savings of $25 off future purchases of Harlequin® and Silhouette® books, AND a 15-minute phone card to call the ones you love, anywhere in North America.

Please send this form, along with your cash register receipts
as proofs of purchase, to:
In the USA: Harlequin Books, P.O. Box 9057, Buffalo, NY 14269-9057
In Canada: Harlequin Books, P.O. Box 622, Fort Erie, Ontario L2A 5X3
Cash register receipts must be dated no later than December 31, 2001.
Limit of 1 coupon booklet and phone card per household.
Please allow 4-6 weeks for delivery.

**I accept your offer! Enclosed are 4 proofs of purchase.
Please send me my coupon booklet
and a 15-minute phone card:**

Name: _____

Address: _____ City: _____

State/Prov.: _____ Zip/Postal Code: _____

Account Number (if available): _____

---

097 KJB DAGL
PHQ4013

If you enjoyed what you just read,
then we've got an offer you can't resist!

Take 2 bestselling
love stories FREE!
Plus get a FREE surprise gift!

Clip this page and mail it to Silhouette Reader Service™

IN U.S.A.	IN CANADA
3010 Walden Ave.	P.O. Box 609
P.O. Box 1867	Fort Erie, Ontario
Buffalo, N.Y. 14240-1867	L2A 5X3

YES! Please send me 2 free Silhouette Special Edition® novels and my free surprise gift. After receiving them, if I don't wish to receive anymore, I can return the shipping statement marked cancel. If I don't cancel, I will receive 6 brand-new novels every month, before they're available in stores! In the U.S.A., bill me at the bargain price of $3.80 plus 25¢ shipping and handling per book and applicable sales tax, if any*. In Canada, bill me at the bargain price of $4.21 plus 25¢ shipping and handling per book and applicable taxes**. That's the complete price and a savings of at least 10% off the cover prices—what a great deal! I understand that accepting the 2 free books and gift places me under no obligation ever to buy any books. I can always return a shipment and cancel at any time. Even if I never buy another book from Silhouette, the 2 free books and gift are mine to keep forever.

235 SEN DFNN
335 SEN DFNP

Name	(PLEASE PRINT)	
Address	Apt.#	
City	State/Prov.	Zip/Postal Code

* Terms and prices subject to change without notice. Sales tax applicable in N.Y.
** Canadian residents will be charged applicable provincial taxes and GST.
 All orders subject to approval. Offer limited to one per household and not valid to current Silhouette Special Edition® subscribers.
 ® are registered trademarks of Harlequin Enterprises Limited.

SPED01 ©1998 Harlequin Enterprises Limited

Silhouette

INTIMATE MOMENTS™
is proud to present

Romancing
the Crown

*With the help of their powerful allies,
the royal family of Montebello is determined
to find their missing heir. But the search for the
beloved prince is not without danger—or passion!*

**This exciting twelve-book series begins in January and
continues throughout the year with these fabulous titles:**

January	(IM #1124)	THE MAN WHO WOULD BE KING by Linda Turner
February	(IM #1130)	THE PRINCESS AND THE MERCENARY by Marilyn Pappano
March	(IM #1136)	THE DISENCHANTED DUKE by Marie Ferrarella
April	(IM #1142)	SECRET-AGENT SHEIK by Linda Winstead Jones
May	(IM #1148)	VIRGIN SEDUCTION by Kathleen Creighton
June	(IM #1154)	ROYAL SPY by Valerie Parv
July	(IM #1160)	HER LORD PROTECTOR by Eileen Wilks
August	(IM #1166)	SECRETS OF A PREGNANT PRINCESS by Carla Cassidy
September	(IM #1172)	A ROYAL MURDER by Lyn Stone
October	(IM #1178)	SARAH'S KNIGHT by Mary McBride
November	(IM #1184)	UNDER THE KING'S COMMAND by Ingrid Weaver
December	(IM #1190)	THE PRINCE'S WEDDING by Justine Davis

Available at your favorite retail outlet.

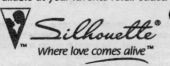

Silhouette®
Where love comes alive™

Visit Silhouette at www.eHarlequin.com

SIMRC